HOW AN
AIRPORT
REALLY WORKS

HOW AN
AIRPORT
REALLY WORKS

GEORGE SULLIVAN

LODESTAR BOOKS
Dutton   New York

Acknowledgments

This author is grateful to many individuals who helped in the preparation of this book. Not only did they contribute information and photographs, but several checked portions of the book for accuracy. Special thanks are due the following: Art Kosatka, Airport Operators Council; Fraser Jones and Duncan Pardue, Federal Aviation Administration; Gene Hathaway and Julie Campbell, National Weather Service; Curtis Dennis, Capt. Stephen Brown, Melba Davis, and Mary Ann Chappers, Port Authority of New York and New Jersey; Kathi Travers, ASPCA; Mary Sue Hartman, United Airlines; Robert Cullen, Barry Kennedy, and Dave Gibb, USAir; Lavonda Walton, U.S. Fish and Wildlife Service; Robert P. Rosscoe, Air Traffic Manager, LaGuardia Airport; Charles Garrett, Garrett Electronics; Tracy L. Trigg-Peters and Joe Esmerado, Chelsea Caterers; Paul T. MacAlester, Hillsborough County (Florida) Aviation Authority; David K. Wilson, Hartsfield Atlanta International Airport; Chuck Cannon, Denver International Airport; Phil Orlandella, Massport; Timothy F. Teeboom, City of Los Angeles, Department of Airports; James E. Anderson, Lindbergh Field, San Diego; Kim Metz, Charlotte/Douglas International Airport; Francesca Kurti, TLC Labs; and Fred Maass, LaGuardia Airport.

Library of Congress Cataloging-in-Publication Data

Sullivan, George.
 How an airport really works/George Sullivan.—1st ed.
  p. cm.
 Includes index.
 Summary: Examines all aspects of what goes on behind the scenes at an airport, exploring such topics as how metal-detectors work and how airplane meals are planned.
 ISBN 0-525-67378-4
 1. Airports—Juvenile literature. [1. Airports.] I. Title.
TL725.S86   1993
387.7'36—dc20   92-20154
                                              CIP
                                               AC

Published in the United States by Lodestar Books,
an affiliate of Dutton Children's Books,
a division of Penguin Books USA Inc.,
375 Hudson Street, New York, New York 10014

Published simultaneously in Canada
by McClelland & Stewart, Toronto

Editor: Rosemary Brosnan   Designer: Richard Granald
        Printed in the U.S.A.   First Edition
              10 9 8 7 6 5 4 3 2 1

Contents

1

Cities That Never Sleep

Imagine an airport that is twice the size of Manhattan Island, an airport that sits on 53 square miles of land. The airport is so big that it can hold Chicago's O'Hare Airport and Dallas/Fort Worth International, with plenty of room left over.

Imagine an airport that will be able to handle more than 100 million passenger departures and arrivals a year. That would make the airport almost twice as busy as Chicago's O'Hare, which now has the title of "the world's busiest airport."

Imagine an airport whose six runways with their related taxiways and ramps represent a surface area that is equal to a single-lane highway running from New York City to Birmingham, Alabama, or from Los Angeles to Spokane, Washington—a distance of just over nine hundred miles.

Imagine an airport that was totally designed and constructed by computers and is now managed by them.

1

Such an airport is no dream. It is the new Denver International Airport.

The United States has some seventeen thousand airports. Of this number, some five hundred serve the scheduled airlines, the airlines that fly planes over specific routes on fixed schedules. They are known as air carrier airports.

These airports are available to business, charter, and private planes. They are the backbone of commercial aviation in the United States.

Denver International, built to replace the city's Stapleton International Airport, is the largest and most modern of the nation's air carrier airports. It is called "the first airport of the twenty-first century."

Basically, an airport is a place where aircraft can take off and land on hard-surfaced landing strips. It has a glass-enclosed tower where air traffic is controlled, a weather station, a terminal area, and facilities for handling baggage and cargo. There are huge hangars where planes are worked upon and stored.

But airports are not just for airplanes; they're for people, too.

More than one hundred thousand passengers a day move through such airports as O'Hare in Chicago, Dallas/Fort Worth International, Hartsfield Atlanta International, and Los Angeles International. And if there are one hundred thousand passengers, there are at least two hundred fifty thousand bags.

With all those people passing through them, airports have to provide the things air travelers want. Airport terminals offer full-service restaurants, coffee shops, and snack bars providing delicatessen-style sandwiches, ice cream, yogurt,

Denver International Airport has been called "the first airport of the twenty-first century." *(Denver International Airport)*

fruit, and nuts. There are gift shops, newsstands, bookstores, and baggage lockers. There is also likely to be a video arcade.

A traveler who has just arrived from a foreign country may want to exchange his or her currency—whether it be pounds or francs, marks or yen—for dollars. Currency exchange is one of the banking services that major airports offer. There are sure to be facilities for photocopying and facsimile transmission, or fax. Postal services are available, too.

For handicapped travelers, there are wheelchairs and special shuttle buses. There's likely to be a Travelers' Aid, the social service agency that assists passengers in need.

Planes line up for takeoff at Seattle/Tacoma International Airport.
(Port of Seattle)

Many airport operations go on behind the scenes. Big-city airports have several fire stations. Million-pound jetliners loaded with a volatile fuel and thundering down runways at tremendous speeds are a constant hazard. Should an accident occur, fire fighters are trained to respond fast—to get to the farthest part of the airport in less than three minutes—to rescue endangered passengers and suppress the fire.

Any major airport has its own police force, too. As a busy transportation center, an airport is bound to attract a few criminals. Baggage theft and pickpocketing are standard airport problems. "Beware of someone telling you that you have a spot on the back of your clothing," says a travel-tip booklet from Dallas/Fort Worth Airport. "Chances are his two accomplices are getting away with your suitcase while you're checking your clothing."

4

Any major airport has to have a heating-and-cooling plant big enough to provide warmth and air-conditioning for fifty thousand people.

Few travelers are ever aware of it, but airports also have fuel farms, huge storage areas where millions of gallons of jet fuel are kept in reserve for delivery to aircraft. At some airports, the fuel storage tanks are above ground; at others, they're buried underground.

The big-city airport boasts a medical center to provide first aid 24 hours a day. Doctors and nurses might be called

It can be underground or aboveground, but every airport has to have a fuel storage area. This is the fuel farm at New York's LaGuardia Airport. *(George Sullivan)*

25 Busiest Airports, U.S. and Canada*

	AIRPORTS	PASSENGER DEPARTURES AND ARRIVALS	AIRCRAFT TAKEOFFS AND LANDINGS
1	Chicago O'Hare International	59,936,137	810,865
2	Dallas/Fort Worth International	48,515,464	731,036
3	Hartsfield Atlanta International	48,024,566	790,502
4	Los Angeles International	45,810,221	679,861
5	San Francisco International	31,059,820	430,253
6	John F. Kennedy International (New York)	29,786,657	302,038
7	Stapleton International (Denver)	27,432,989	484,040
8	Miami International	25,837,445	480,987
9	Honolulu International	23,367,770	407,048
10	Logan International (Boston)	22,935,844	424,568
11	LaGuardia (New York)	22,753,812	354,229
12	Detroit Metropolitan Wayne County	22,585,156	387,848
13	Newark International	22,255,002	379,432
14	Sky Harbor International (Phoenix)	21,718,068	498,752
15	Minneapolis-St. Paul International	20,381,314	379,785
16	Lester B. Pearson International (Toronto)	20,304,271	353,682
17	St. Louis-Lambert International	20,065,737	439,002
18	Las Vegas McCarran International	18,618,781	400,680
19	Orlando International	18,397,830	281,947
20	Houston Intercontinental	17,518,791	314,436
21	Greater-Pittsburgh International	17,145,831	385,837
22	Philadelphia International	16,290,201	407,363
23	Seattle/Tacoma International	16,240,309	355,007
24	Charlotte/Douglas International	15,614,285	418,385
25	Washington National Airport	15,569,933	313,740

* Source: Airport Operators Council International, 1990

25 Busiest Foreign Airports*

	AIRPORT	PASSENGER DEPARTURES AND ARRIVALS	AIRCRAFT TAKEOFFS AND LANDINGS
1	London Heathrow (England)	42,964,200	390,485
2	Tokyo International/Haneda (Japan)	40,233,031	183,950
3	Frankfurt-Main International (Germany)	28,912,145	324,387
4	Paris Orly (France)	24,329,700	193,451
5	Osaka International (Japan)	23,511,611	130,550
6	Paris Charles De Gaulle (France)	22,506,107	235,350
7	London Gatwick (England)	21,185,400	203,200
8	New Tokyo International/Narita (Japan)	19,264,650	125,187
9	Hong Kong International (Hong Kong)	18,687,525	122,945
10	Aeroporti di Roma (Italy)	17,835,885	176,456
11	Amsterdam Schiphol (Netherlands)	16,185,810	245,350
12	Stockholm Arlanda (Sweden)	14,821,692	257,606
13	Singapore Changi (Singapore)	14,403,580	97,675
14	Bangkok International (Thailand)	14,329,337	125,998
15	Fukuoka/Itazuke (Japan)	13,227,659	86,820
16	Zurich International (Switzerland)	12,694,507	219,329
17	Copenhagen Kastrup (Denmark)	12,460,090	212,713
18	Sydney (Australia)	12,223,106	194,065
19	Dusseldorf (Germany)	11,575,493	155,029
20	Munich International (Germany)	11,218,119	191,856
21	Manchester International (England)	10,816,522	152,554
22	Milan Linate (Italy)	9,335,361	135,396
23	Chiang Kai-shek International (Taiwan)	8,929,218	56,539
24	San Juan Luís Muñoz Marin International (Puerto Rico)	8,724,744	204,994
25	Bombay Sahar International (India)	8,454,362	67,123

* Source: Airport Operators Council International, 1990

upon to treat a child who catches a finger in a baggage carousel or an elderly woman who stumbles on an escalator
and gashes an arm.

But they also have to be prepared for the unexpected. A
nurse at O'Hare had to leave off treating frostbite cases on
one of the coldest days in Chicago's history to apply oint-
ment to the legs of a young man returning from a vacation
in the Bahamas with second-degree sunburn.

To many travelers, airports are just places to check in for
a flight, kill time, and board planes. They may buy a news-
paper or have a quick snack. They're unaware that major
airports are like cities. They operate 24 hours a day, 7 days
a week, 365 days a year, providing a tremendous array of
services. But unlike some cities, airports are cities always on
the move; an airport never sleeps.

OTHER TYPES OF AIRPORTS

More than eleven thousand airports in the United States are
classified as general aviation airports. They serve all types of
aircraft, except those of the scheduled airlines.

Small aircraft use general aviation airports. These aircraft
include business and private aircraft, as well as the small
planes used in flight instruction, aerial photography, and
crop dusting.

In addition to the air carrier and general aviation airports
in the United States, the armed forces operate between four
hundred and five hundred airports. Military airports range
in size from small fields for light planes to huge airports
with runways two miles long, and longer, for fast jet fighters
and huge bombers.

General aviation airports serve all types of planes, except those of scheduled airlines. *(Federal Aviation Administration)*

All United States and foreign airports have been assigned a three-letter identifier code by the International Air Transport Association. Chicago's O'Hare Airport is designated ORD; Dallas/Fort Worth is DFW; and Los Angeles is LAX. (Other identifier codes are listed on pages 10 and 11.)

The next time you travel by air and check a piece of baggage, look at the tag the clerk attaches to it. It bears the identifier code for the airport that is your destination.

LOOKING BACK

Aviation pioneers of the early part of the century could scarcely have imagined anything to compare with the modern big-city airport. When Orville and Wilbur Wright

Airport Identifier Codes, U.S. and Canada

AIRPORT	CODE
Charlotte/Douglas International	CLT
Chicago O'Hare International	ORD
Dallas/Fort Worth International	DFW
Detroit Metropolitan Wayne County	DTW
Greater-Pittsburgh International	PIT
Hartsfield Atlanta International	ATL
Honolulu International	HNL
Houston Intercontinental	IAH
John F. Kennedy International (New York)	JFK
LaGuardia (New York)	LGA
Las Vegas McCarran International	LAS
Lester B. Pearson International (Toronto)	YYZ
Logan International (Boston)	BOS
Los Angeles International	LAX
Miami International	MIA
Minneapolis-St. Paul International	MSP
Newark International	EWR
Orlando International	ORL
Philadelphia International	PHL
St. Louis-Lambert International	STL
San Francisco International	SFO
Seattle/Tacoma International	SEA
Sky Harbor International (Phoenix)	PHX
Stapleton International (Denver)	DEN
Washington National Airport	DCA

Airport Identifier Codes, Foreign Airports

AIRPORT	CODE
Aeroporti di Roma (Italy)	FCO
Amsterdam Schiphol (Netherlands)	AMS
Bangkok International (Thailand)	BKK
Bombay Sahar International (India)	BOM
Chiang Kai-shek International (Taiwan)	TPE
Copenhagen Kastrup (Denmark)	CPH
Dusseldorf (Germany)	DUS
Frankfurt-Main International (Germany)	FRA
Fukuoka/Itazuke (Japan)	FUK
Hong Kong International (Hong Kong)	HKG
London Gatwick (England)	LGW
London Heathrow (England)	LHR
Manchester International (England)	MAN
Milan Linate (Italy)	LIN
Munich International (Germany)	MUC
New Tokyo International/Narita (Japan)	NRT
Osaka International (Japan)	OSA
Paris Charles De Gaulle (France)	CDG
Paris Orly (France)	ORY
San Juan Luís Muñoz Marin International (Puerto Rico)	SJU
Singapore Changi (Singapore)	SIN
Stockholm Arlanda (Sweden)	STO
Sydney (Australia)	SYD
Tokyo International/Haneda (Japan)	HND
Zurich International (Switzerland)	ZRH

succeeded in achieving true manned and powered flight near Kitty Hawk, North Carolina, on December 17, 1903, the place where they took off from was no airport. It was merely the gentle slope of a big sand dune on a long and narrow coastal island.

In the years that followed, as the number of planes kept increasing, it became clear that they needed a place to land and take off, a place where they could be fueled, worked on, and sheltered from bad weather. Airplanes needed airports.

While records indicate that airports were in operation as early as 1909, they were hardly recognizable as such. They had no paved runways, no terminal buildings. They were simply meadows, parks, or athletic fields with room enough for a plane to operate. They were called landing fields.

By 1912, there were 20 airports in the country. World War I, which broke out in Europe in 1914, stirred the U.S. Army's interest in airplanes. The United States entered the war in 1917. During the conflict, which ended in 1918, 67 military airports were built.

The years between World War I and World War II were a period of exciting growth for aviation. Commercial airlines, operating aircraft to carry people and cargo, had their beginnings after World War I. There were aircraft left over from the war that could be used as passenger planes, and there were plenty of trained pilots available to fly them.

Scores of municipal airports were opened to serve the airlines. At the same time, the U.S. Army sought airports for its fighter planes and bombers. The Post Office Department needed them for its Air Mail service.

By 1921, there were 271 airports in the United States. By 1927, the number had jumped to 1,036.

In the late 1920s, the terminal at San Francisco's airport, now the nation's fifth busiest, looked like this. *(San Francisco International Airport)*

In the early 1940s, when air travel was still a bit unusual, passengers on Reading (Pennsylvania) Airways were given this ticket as a souvenir of their flight.
(*George Sullivan*)

Many of the problems that are now associated with airports date to this period. That's because planners were unable to foresee the rapid growth of air travel. No one could even imagine the era of huge jets, aircraft able to carry passengers by the hundreds.

Wooden planes of the 1920s and 1930s were tiny when compared to today's giant aircraft. The few passengers they carried often had to be wedged in among mailbags. About all one needed for an airport was a flat and open area, enough room for a single runway.

On the outskirts of most cities there was plenty of land available, and it was relatively cheap. People didn't worry about engine noise. Airplanes of the time didn't operate with a thunderous roar; they merely clattered.

Pollution? Not in the 1920s. It would be almost half a century before people would begin to use that word in connection with the exhaust fumes from airplane engines.

The airplane represented exciting fun in the 1920s and 1930s. As recreation, families would sometimes drive out to the local airport on a Sunday afternoon. They'd park near the runway and watch planes land and take off. The future had arrived!

People wanted airports for their cities. To be included on the route of a scheduled airline was something like having a major league baseball franchise today. An airport gave a city status.

The Civil Aeronautics Act, which became law in 1938, provided for the further development of airports for commercial use. The Act also established the Civil Aeronautics Board (CAB) to regulate airline fares, routes, and schedules.

AIRPORT PROBLEMS

The years that followed World War II saw more surging growth in commercial aviation. The jet age arrived in the 1950s. Planes could fly faster than ever before.

They could also carry more people. In the early 1960s, the biggest airliners carried one hundred fifty passengers. The first jumbo jet, the Boeing 747, which several airlines began to use in the 1970s, could carry close to five hundred passengers. Other big jets followed the Boeing 747.

In 1978, the Airline Deregulation Act was passed by Congress and signed by President Jimmy Carter. The law relaxed the federal government's control of airline routes and fares. Many new airlines offering discount fares set up shop. Air travel boomed.

As aircraft got bigger, longer runways were needed. But often there was no room to expand.

As the number of air travelers grew by leaps and bounds, the nation's airports failed to keep pace. Air traffic facilities became overtaxed, resulting in delays in takeoffs and landings. "You Can Fly, You Just Can't Land" was the title of an article that appeared in *Travel Weekly* in 1985.

Airports also suffered from clogged highways linking them with the cities they served. Passengers often found it very difficult getting to and from the airports. Missed flights were sometimes the result.

The jet age triggered another problem—noise pollution. A woman who lives near Boston's Logan Airport says the scream of jet engines "is like standing next to a motorcycle

North and South Terminals at Hartsfield Atlanta International Airport, the largest passenger terminal complex in the world *(Hartsfield Atlanta International Airport)*

revving at full throttle." The Federal Aviation Administration (FAA) and the Environmental Protection Agency (EPA) set limits for airport noise.

Some of the nation's newer airports—Denver International, Dallas/Fort Worth International, and Hartsfield Atlanta International—have sought to solve these problems. They've built outside of the boundaries of the cities they serve. Jet engines annoy fewer people.

Their runway and terminal complexes have been designed to handle an ever-increasing number of air travelers with ease and efficiency. Speedy ground transportation is available between the airport and the inner city.

Perhaps these airports signal what airports of the future will be like, and people will enjoy visiting airports again, just as they did more than half a century ago.

2

Planning and Design

In the United States, cities, counties, or public corporations own most major airports. Small airports, on the other hand, are usually privately owned.

When the local government agrees that a new airport is needed or wishes to expand an existing airport, it first has to decide how much money to spend. The next question is how to raise that money—through taxes or by borrowing through the sale of revenue bonds. Perhaps the federal government will agree to underwrite part of the cost.

Of course, the operating authority looks forward to the airport making a profit, or at least being self-supporting. An airport gets its income from two principal sources—traffic operations and concessions.

Traffic operations include the landing fees the airlines pay; the rent the airport receives for hangars, gates, and terminal space; and the sale of fuel and oil.

Concessions cover just about everything else, including the money received from restaurants, snack bars, bookstores,

The Main Terminal at Washington's Dulles International Airport, designed by architect Eero Saarinen, is a dramatic sight. *(Federal Aviation Administration)*

souvenir shops, car parking, car rental, and even the coin-operated television sets that cost 25 cents for half an hour of viewing.

CHOOSING A SITE

At the same time they're wrestling with money matters, the local government is likely to hire a firm that specializes in airport planning. The planners start by choosing a location for the airport.

Modern-day airports require much more land than those of earlier days. One reason is because airplanes are so much bigger and more powerful. The biggest jets require two or more miles of runway when landing or taking off. Airports also have to be of tremendous size to be able to absorb the noise of landings and takeoffs.

Noise, in fact, is the biggest objection people have to airports. The ear splitting cry of jet engines—described by a New Jersey resident as "like that of a city bus roaring through my bedroom"—is bad enough. But it is also what that noise implies.

Westchester County (New York) Airport is close to a large development of single-family homes. Early in 1981, a corporate jet crashed while taking off from the airport. "When an airplane is flying overhead," says a Westchester County official, "the noise makes people unconsciously feel they are in danger."

When Dallas/Fort Worth International opened in 1974, it was, with an area of about 17,500 acres, the largest airport in the United States. Denver International, which is more than twice the size of Dallas/Fort Worth, is now the nation's biggest.

The world's largest is King Khalid International Airport near Riyadh, Saudi Arabia. It covers 55,040 acres, which is about a hundred square miles, an area about one-tenth the size of Rhode Island.

Once the location has been agreed upon, airport planners prepare a land-use plan that covers the airport and the area surrounding it. The plan establishes the layout of the runways, taxiways, terminal area, and other buildings, and the size of each.

Land uses for areas surrounding the airport are often controlled through zoning, that is, by setting building restrictions. Zoning puts a limit on the height of buildings close to the airport. Any tall building would present a hazard to low-flying planes.

Most planners like to have recreational areas next to their airport. Parks and golf courses are considered good neighbors. But planners shun landfills and dumps, which attract birds that can be a hazard to planes. Ponds and lakes also draw birds, chiefly wildfowl. They may have to be filled in.

At Denver International Airport, design and construction were managed by computers. The computers allowed architects and engineers to develop solutions to day-to-day construction problems. For instance, officials of Continental Airlines were dissatisfied when shown plans for their terminal at Denver International. The company asked that its terminal be moved a few hundred feet to allow more parking spaces for aircraft. The specifications for the new terminal were fed into the computer, which then spewed out the new construction drawings and engineering data.

THE RUNWAYS

While the city or local operating authority has a free hand in planning the airport's ground facilities, the federal government, through the Federal Aviation Administration, oversees the design and construction of all navigation services. Mainly these include the runways, taxiways, and loading ramps, plus any facilities relating to air traffic control.

An airport's runways, the long strips on which planes land and take off, can be laid out in several different ways. In fact, the FAA describes 22 different runway layouts in a circular it makes available to airport planners.

ABOVE: **Parallel runways at Seattle/Tacoma International Airport run in a north-south direction.** *(The Port of Seattle)*

ABOVE RIGHT: **Runways at San Diego's Lindbergh Field intersect to form a V.** *(Port of San Diego)*

RIGHT: **Runways are marked by compass headings. This runway, designated 28, points in the direction of 280 degrees, or 10 degrees north of due west.** *(Federal Aviation Administration)*

The single runway is the simplest design. Planes use it for both landing and taking off.

Many small airports are single-runway operations. In some cases, the runway may be merely a strip of mowed grass, only two thousand to twenty-five hundred feet in length.

A single-runway airport operates with great efficiency, since it has many fewer air traffic control problems than an airport with several runways laid out in different directions. When the weather is good, a single-runway airport can easily handle planes at the rate of one a minute.

But a single runway has serious disadvantages. Any runway mishap—a plane sliding off the edge, for instance—means the airport has to shut down until the aircraft has been removed. Resurfacing the runway can mean suspending airport operations for several days.

Major airports have several runways. A second runway parallel to the first can just about double the number of planes an airport can handle. It makes untimely airport shutdowns much less likely to happen.

A very busy airport might have two pairs of parallel runways, with as much as a mile of spacing in between. They're called dual-lane runways.

In planning runways, the prevailing winds are a matter of critical importance. An airplane should land and take off while heading into the wind. This assures the plane the greatest possible lift. Increased lift means the plane gets up into the air faster. It also makes for greater stability during landings. If the prevailing winds in a community blow out of the north, the main airport runways will be laid out in a north-south direction.

Crosswinds also have to be considered. They can be a real hazard to a plane landing or taking off.

Crosswinds are the main reason that some airports use intersecting runways. Intersecting runways are those that cross one another. From the air, they look like a **V** or an **X**.

When strong winds are blowing out of the north, an airport may be forced to shut down its east-west runways. It can continue to use its north-south runways, however. When winds are relatively light, all runways can be used.

The sprawling Dallas/Fort Worth International Airport has six runways. Four are laid out on a north-south axis, and two others run diagonally to these, in a northwest-southeast direction. Crosswinds never cause Dallas/Fort Worth to close down.

Huge white numbers are painted at the opposite ends of the runway to serve as a navigational aid to pilots. The numbers tell the compass direction in which the runway is laid out. For example, a runway with an 18 and 36 painted on it is a north-south runway. The 18 (an abbreviation for 180°) appears on the runway's north end. The 36 (for 360°) is at the south end.

Airport planning and design must also include the means of getting aircraft from the runways to the terminal gates. This is accomplished with taxiways. At major airports, each runway is served by a pair of taxiways, which run parallel to it. This system enables aircraft to move to and from the same runway at the same time.

Turnoffs are located at the end of each runway and at right angles to it. Turnoffs are short strips of concrete or asphalt that link the runway to the taxiway. They're also called exit taxiways.

In the case of busy runways, turnoffs are located at sev-

To passengers, terminals are the place where they buy their tickets or check in. The scene above is at the Anchorage (Alaska) International Airport. *(Anchorage International Airport)*

eral points. This makes it possible for a plane to leave the runway as soon as possible after it has slowed down or stopped, so the next plane can land or take off.

TERMINALS

The terminal area is the part of the airport most familiar to passengers. It is there that flights begin and end.

It is where departing passengers purchase their tickets or have previously purchased tickets verified. Passengers also check their baggage, while arriving passengers claim their baggage.

At one part of the terminal complex at the Tampa (Florida) International Airport, vehicle access roads approach the terminal at several different levels. *(Federal Aviation Administration)*

Airport planners look at terminals in an unusual way. To the planners, the terminal is a building or an area where the passenger makes the transfer from air transportation to ground transportation, or vice versa. Their goal is to design a terminal that allows this to happen with a minimum of delay and confusion.

Planners may recommend a single terminal building or a complex of terminals. At Dallas/Fort Worth, for instance, passengers choose from one of four terminals, depending on the airline they're using. American Airlines and Delta Airlines each have their own terminals. Each of the other two terminals are shared by several airlines. The four terminals provide gate positions for more than a hundred aircraft.

Terminal planners assume that the passenger is making his or her first flight and has never visited the terminal before. Simple signs have been developed to direct the passenger to the right airline ticket counter, or anywhere else he or she wants to go. But because most airports today are used by people of different nationalities, the signs express basic information in pictographs—pictures that represent words—rather than in a particular language.

Developed by the U.S. Department of Transportation, these pictographs help guide travelers, many of whom may not speak English, at airline terminals. Left to right, top row: water fountain, men's room, duty-free gifts, telephones, women's room; middle row: information, lockers, elevators, no smoking, hotel information; bottom row: customs, currency exchange, lost and found, first aid, restaurant. *(Department of Transportation)*

In fact, the U.S. Department of Transportation has developed a uniform system of pictographs for use in airports. Some of these are shown on page 27.

MOVING PEOPLE

Since a modern-day airport can cover as much area as a good-sized city, airport planners have to be concerned about how to move people around inside the terminal area. How do you get passengers from the check-in counters to their departure gates when it's too far to walk? And what about the traveler who has to switch airlines? How do you get that passenger from one terminal to another?

Buses used to be a standard method of moving passengers around airports. And at some older airports, they still are. If you're at Washington National Airport, which opened in 1941, and you want to get from the Main Terminal to the North Terminal, you wait for the free shuttle bus.

But there are better systems. At Tampa International Airport in Florida, a monorail system connects each of the four terminals to the main terminal. Riding the elevated concrete trackway are electrically powered 125-passenger coaches, each of which is computer controlled.

The Tampa Airport transit system is capable of moving as many as three thousand passengers from the main terminal to their airplanes in ten minutes. Each passenger's journey takes about 40 seconds.

At the Dallas/Fort Worth Airport, passengers also ride a monorail system, known as Airtrans. An on-board computer controls each of the 40-passenger rubber-tired cars that travel on an elevated concrete guideway. A computer-

At Tampa International, a monorail system connects the airport's four terminal buildings. *(Tampa International Airport)*

generated voice tells passengers when they are about to reach their destinations.

The Airtrans system not only links the airport's four terminals, it also speeds passengers to outlying points around the airport—to parking lots, rental car facilities, and an airport hotel.

Another way of getting passengers to their aircraft is the mobile lounge, a system that is used at Dulles International Airport near Washington, D.C. Passengers go directly from the check-in counter to a rectangular-shaped, enclosed waiting area that is mounted on a four-wheeled chassis. It has room for about one hundred fifty passengers.

When the aircraft is ready for boarding, the vehicle is

Dulles International Airport offers mobile lounges to move passengers.
(Federal Aviation Administration)

driven onto the loading apron. The section can be elevated to the level needed to load passengers onto the aircraft. Its doors connect with the aircraft's doors.

One advantage of the mobile lounge is that it eliminates the need for waiting lounges within the terminal building. This makes for a smaller terminal built at a lower cost.

Airports also get people from one place to another with moving walkways, which operate on the same principle as a conveyor belt. The passenger can either stand still or walk.

Hartsfield Atlanta International Airport, which boasts the world's largest terminal complex, offers travelers a choice. The complex is huge, covering an area equal to 45 football fields. It is made up of two terminals set at right angles to four concourses where domestic flights are boarded, plus an international concourse.

The two terminals and five concourses are linked by an underground mall. Passengers can walk, travel by means of a moving sidewalk, or board a transit system. The system's vehicles are automatically guided to stations within the concourses at two-minute intervals. The longest trip is only five minutes. There's no charge to riders.

Planners have to provide ramps and roadways alongside terminal buildings, where buses, limousines, private cars, and taxis pick up and drop off passengers. Dallas/Fort Worth International, Miami International, and many other big-city airports provide links with mass transportation systems.

OTHER SERVICES

While virtually all passenger flights carry mail and other freight besides baggage, most major airports require separate terminals for aircraft that haul cargo. Electronic goods and machine parts are often shipped by air. So are perishables— flowers, fish, fruits, and vegetables. Important documents, such as checks, stocks, and bonds, frequently go by air, too.

New York's John F. Kennedy International and Los Angeles International are the leading cargo airports in the United States. Each handles more than a million tons of cargo a year. Chicago's O'Hare and Miami International handle almost that much.

Airport planners have to decide how much hangar space the cargo carriers will need. They need storage areas and access roads for their trucks.

Major airports also have to provide facilities for the planes not operated by the scheduled airlines. These include both business aircraft and private aircraft, which often account for as much as 10 percent of the traffic at air carrier airports.

3

Terminal Operations

The busy terminal complex is the part of the airport most familiar to air travelers. It is usually placed at the very heart of the airport, with satellite buildings surrounding it.

The terminal is not only the hub of passenger activities. It is the airport's nerve center, with a wide range of activities going on behind the scenes.

From the offices within the terminal, the airport manager and the management staff supervise the airport's operation. They work with the various airlines that have terminal and gate space at the airport, seeking to provide both safety and efficiency.

When residents of the local community complain about noise, their complaints are likely to fall upon the ears of the airport manager. Working with air traffic control officials and the airlines, he or she may have runway assignments rotated so aircraft are not taking off over the same homes every time. Or he or she may be able to prevail upon pilots not to apply full throttle until the planes are well up in the air.

The airport manager and the management staff oversee the maintenance crews that help keep the runways in first class operating condition. They supervise the men and women who clean and care for the various airport buildings and they're in charge of the airport's crash, fire, and rescue teams, discussed in chapter 4.

The terminal also contains an operations center for each airline that uses the airport. Here pilots receive flight information. Captains are given a flight plan that outlines the route the flight is to take and a loadsheet showing the plane's weight and balance. They also get a report on the amount of fuel that is needed for the flight as well as weather information.

The airline's dispatch office handles all pre-departure planning. Dispatchers keep aware of the weather, schedule changes, and other factors. Even when a flight is in the air, a dispatcher can reroute a plane, should the weather or other conditions make it necessary.

At ticket counters within the terminal, departing passengers, often struggling with their baggage, purchase their tickets or have their tickets verified. At the same time, they check their baggage.

BAGGAGE HANDLING

Baggage is weighed at the time it is checked. In days past, airlines also weighed each passenger because weight was a critical matter in the case of early aircraft, which were much less powerful than today's jets. Nowadays, airlines simply figure an average weight for each passenger.

Once a piece of luggage is weighed and checked, it is

carried to a sorting area by means of a moving belt located behind the counter. There the baggage for many different flights is loaded onto carts to be towed to the aircraft.

United Airlines was the first to install a high-tech baggage sorting system. It's to be found at the United terminal at Chicago's O'Hare Airport. As a bag travels down the conveyor, its coded identification tag is scanned by six different lasers. Big paddles then push each bag toward the right flight. The system can sort 480 bags a minute.

With most planes, baggage is carried in a cargo hold that is located beneath the floor of the airplane. Bags, along with cargo, freight, and mail, are loaded into the hold by means of an inclined conveyor belt that is mounted on the chassis of a small truck.

In recent years, there has been a trend toward pre-packing baggage for a particular flight into removable containers that fit into the plane's fuselage. The container system is used on the Boeing 747, Boeing 767, and Lockheed L1011.

When a plane arrives at its destination, the sequence is reversed. The baggage is taken from the aircraft and delivered to the terminal's baggage-claim area. There it is placed on a conveyor belt or a circular revolving platform, called a carousel, to be claimed by the passengers.

Once passengers have had their tickets verified and their baggage checked, they make their way to a terminal gate for boarding. At a major airport, there may be a hundred or more gates. When Denver International Airport opened, it had 97 gates in operation. The airport plans to have 200 gates when fully developed.

At the gate, ticketing agents check each passenger's name against a computerized list. Then passengers are given a

Cargo containers, which fit snugly into a plane's cargo hold, make baggage handling quicker and easier. This container is from a Boeing 767. *(Federal Aviation Administration)*

boarding pass that, along with their ticket, allows them to board the plane.

TURNAROUND

Passengers at ticket counters or gates may not realize that the plane they are waiting for may not yet have completed its previous flight. It could still be in the sky, many miles from the airport.

Once the plane lands, the captain, under the direction of the control tower, guides the plane through the airport's system of taxiways to its assigned gate. Nearing the gate, the captain keeps the plane's nosewheel on a particular yellow line painted on the concrete. The captain also gets hand signals from a line person, usually one of the airline mechanics. When line persons cross their arms over their head, it's a signal to apply the brakes; the plane is lined up properly with the jetway, the telescoping walkway that links the plane with the terminal.

A telescoping jetway connects a plane to the terminal. This is the Detroit Metropolitan Airport. *(Detroit Metropolitan Airport; Jean Manning)*

A line person directs a plane into the terminal gate. *(George Sullivan)*

At LaGuardia and other airports where room to maneuver is limited, tugs tow each plane into its assigned gate. *(George Sullivan)*

As soon as the plane comes to a stop, a mechanic places chocks at the wheels to prevent the plane from rolling. The captain and crew shut the plane down.

At that moment, a thoroughly planned, carefully timed operation involving a dozen or so airline employees gets underway. It's called a turnaround. In a very short span of time, the passengers will leave the aircraft—deplane, it's called—and their baggage and the plane's cargo will be unloaded. The plane's interior will be cleaned, and the plane will be refueled and then loaded with new passengers, their baggage, their meals, cargo, and perhaps mail.

Turnarounds are serious business. Airlines are making money only when their planes are in the air. They don't want them sitting at terminal gates.

Equally important, they want their planes to leave on time because delays frustrate passengers and result in bad feelings toward the airline.

Airlines set strict schedules for terminal turnarounds, depending on the size of the plane and the number of passengers it carries. For instance, USAir, the nation's seventh largest airline, wants its ramp services crews to turn around a Douglas DC-9 in 33 minutes. For the slightly larger Boeing 737, it's 38 minutes.

Even before the flight attendant has opened the airplane's exit door, permitting passengers to stream through the jetway into the terminal, a member of the ramp crew has opened the hatch in the plane's belly and started removing baggage. "We're supposed to get the first bag off within 45 seconds after the plane has arrived at the gate," says Barry Kennedy, a ramp services supervisor for USAir.

Once in a while, a passenger's bag fails to show up in the

baggage-claim area. When that happens, most airlines will, on request, give the passenger enough money to make emergency purchases of a toothbrush, other toilet articles, and some clothing, including a change of underwear. According to the Department of Transportation, 98 percent of all lost bags are eventually found and returned.

As the arriving passengers are leaving the plane at the front exit, the cleaners are likely to be entering at the rear. There are usually two or three of them, depending on the size of the aircraft. One wields a portable vacuum cleaner. Another carries a trash bag and begins to collect the newspapers, magazines, and whatever else the passengers may have left behind. Other cleaners arrive in a lavatory truck to ready the plane's bathrooms for the new passengers.

A galley truck pulls up to the plane. The truck's body is raised to the level of the passenger deck by means of a hydraulically-operated scissors lift. Meals from the flight kitchen are quickly unloaded.

Some airlines operate their own flight kitchens at airports where food is prepared for passengers. Other airlines purchase meals from catering companies. In either case, dieticians plan the meals, and chefs do the cooking.

MEAL PREPARATION

Chelsea Catering Corporation, with kitchens in Denver, Newark, Houston, Los Angeles, and New York (LaGuardia Airport), caters more than two hundred forty thousand flights a year. Much of the company's meal planning is done by computer, by what Chelsea calls its Kitchen Management System. KMS analyzes the menu requirements for each

Meals for passengers arrive in a truck with a body elevated to doorway level by a hydraulically operated scissors lift.
(*George Sullivan*)

flight and determines what foods and beverages will be required. It then reports the items that must be purchased, what activities must be accomplished by each work center in the kitchen, the staff and equipment needed, and the costs involved.

An executive chef heads up each of Chelsea's kitchens. George Pinier, from Angers, France, is the company's executive chef in Los Angeles. He worked previously in restaurants in New York, Florida, and California.

Pinier found the airline catering business to be much different from the restaurant business. "The quantity of food is different," he said. "And you cook to order in a restaurant.

In the airline business, you must always cook in advance."

At the same time meals are going aboard, a drinking-water truck hooks up to the plane. It holds several hundred gallons of water to refill the airplane's water tank.

On the other side of the gate, passengers are getting fidgety. Their flight is scheduled to depart in about 20 minutes.

The turnaround continues. Mechanics clean the plane's windshield and change the oil in the engines. Any mechanical problem reported by the flight crew is corrected. A wing light may need to be replaced, a tire may need to be changed.

The plane is refueled. At some airports, jet fuel is delivered to the aircraft by a huge tank truck. Other airports

BELOW LEFT: **At airports with underground storage tanks, a hydrant cart pumps fuel into aircraft.** (George Sullivan)

BELOW RIGHT: **Fuel is pumped from a fuel truck into the airplane's wing tank.** (United Airlines)

have underground fuel farms, made up of buried tanks in which fuel is stored. At JFK International Airport in New York, the underground fuel farm is capable of storing 32 million gallons of aviation fuel in 102 storage tanks. Computers are used to speed the flow of fuel through the system's 50 miles of underground pipe.

When an aircraft requires fuel, a trucklike vehicle called a hydrant cart is summoned. The driver attaches one end of a thick hose to the nearest underground fuel tank. The other end of the hose hooks into the plane's tanks. The truck then pumps fuel out of storage and into the plane. It usually takes only about 10 minutes to refuel a plane.

At about the same time the first passengers are boarding, tugs arrive at the plane's belly towing dollies with baggage and cargo. "The cargo and mail go in first," says Barry Kennedy of USAir, "and then the baggage. That's so the baggage will be able to come off first when the plane arrives.

"And we have to separate the baggage according to destination. If a plane is going south from New York to Charlotte and then farther south to Birmingham, the Birmingham baggage goes in before the Charlotte baggage."

As the last pieces of baggage are being stacked in the baggage compartment, passengers who have boarded the plane are taking their seats and fastening their seat belts. Once all of the baggage has gone aboard and the compartment has been sealed shut, the airline dispatch office notifies the flight crew that the plane is ready for takeoff. Shortly after, the jetway is retracted. The crew revs up the engines and gets clearance to leave the gate from the control tower; then they back the aircraft out onto the ramp before turning onto the taxiway.

Baggage goes aboard a USAir flight. In the foreground, cargo awaits loading. *(George Sullivan)*

For the turnaround crew, there's no relaxing, however. There's likely to be another plane that needs to be turned around arriving at another gate. In a single eight-hour shift, one ramp crew may service well over one hundred different aircraft.

If a plane happens to be late in leaving its gate, airline officials want to know why. Was it because the caterer was slow in putting meals aboard? Or perhaps it was because the fuel truck arrived late. They study reports to try to find ways to eliminate delays.

The airlines also check the performance of ramp service crews by assigning employees to make flights and report how well the various crew members do their jobs. How long did it take to get the plane into the gate? How long was the wait for baggage? Members of the crews have a special name for such employees. They call them "ghost riders."

4

Behind the Scenes

With the loud ring of the emergency telephone in the communications center at New York's LaGuardia Airport, all routine business halts immediately. A three-engine jet is headed for a landing on Runway 4 with a warning light flashing on the flight deck, the signal that there's a hydraulic pressure problem.

In less than thirty seconds, a big yellow crash, fire, and rescue truck carrying a pair of fire fighters in silvery flame-resistant suits is on its way to the scene. Minutes after, the airplane touches down safely.

The alert, called a 4-2, is over. "We get about one 4-2 a day," says Captain Stephen Brown who heads crash, fire, and rescue operations at LaGuardia.

Occasionally LaGuardia's fire fighters are called upon to answer a 4-3, which implies something more serious than a 4-2. Perhaps there's a problem with the plane's brakes or a flap, one of the hinged control surfaces on the trailing edge of the wing.

45

Airport fire fighters wear traditional bunker coats (left) made of flame-resistant Nomex, double-lined, or heat-resistant aluminized uniforms (right), with a Kevlar and polyester outer shell lined with Nomex. *(George Sullivan)*

A 4-4 is even rarer. That's a "hot emergency"—a crash.

At Dallas/Fort Worth International Airport on August 31, 1988, Delta Airlines 1141, a Boeing 727 with 108 persons aboard, and carrying nearly five thousand gallons of fuel, crashed on takeoff. The aircraft's right wing dipped and struck the ground at the edge of the runway. The wing then broke apart, gushing a trail of fuel as the aircraft skidded for almost three thousand feet. Fire broke out.

When the first crash, fire, and rescue vehicle reached the scene, the plane was engulfed in flames, and no passengers were visible. Immediately the crew began pumping foam onto the burning aircraft. It took several minutes to knock down the flames, but thanks to the speed and skill of the fire fighters, 94 passengers and crew members managed to survive the accident.

Such emergencies seldom occur. In fact, many airport fire fighters go through their entire careers without becoming involved in a serious crash.

Nevertheless, airport fire fighters are prepared for every type of emergency, small or large. Not only are they thoroughly trained, but they operate sophisticated crash, fire, and rescue vehicles.

The first to reach the accident scene is a rapid intervention vehicle, or RIV. Very fast, despite the big load of water, foam concentrate, dry chemical, and medical and rescue equipment it carries, the RIV and its two-person crew seek to keep the fire under control until the main force arrives.

Heavy-duty foam trucks follow the RIVs. Big and also very fast, they can cross the rough terrain between runways to reach the accident scene as quickly as possible. They carry four times as much foam as the RIVs. Their turret-mounted nozzles can swivel beyond 180 degrees, shooting heavy streams of foam or water over distances of up to three hundred feet.

Foam, not water, is preferred in extinguishing aircraft fuel fires. Technically, it is called Aqueous Film Forming Foam, or AFFF. When mixed with water and charged with air within the turret of the emergency vehicle, the foam concentrate expands to ten times its original size.

Poured onto a fire, the foam forms a thick layer of bubbles that works to smother the flames. The foam also cools the surrounding area, preventing the outbreak of other fires.

"The foam we use is something like the liquid detergent used in washing dishes," explains Sergeant Mike Maiorano, one of LaGuardia's fire fighters. "Mix water and detergent and you get a concentration of tiny bubbles. Those bubbles help to eliminate heat and oxygen and suppress the fire."

Foam, not water, is what's used in suppressing aircraft fires. This scene is at a test "burn site." *(Federal Aviation Administration)*

Foam has to be applied in enormous quantities to do the job. Fire fighters seek to create what the National Fire Protection Association calls an "impervious fire-resistant blanket." Then they have to be watchful that the blanket is not torn open by a sudden gust of wind or by water streams from other hoses. A heavy-duty vehicle can pour more than ten thousand gallons of foam a minute onto a fire.

In the case of an emergency alert that involves a plane that has landed and crashed, the fire fighters' chief responsibility is to use their foam to rescue people. That means knocking down the fire so as to create paths to the plane's

A heavy-duty vehicle can pour ten thousand gallons of foam a minute on a fire. *(Oshkosh Truck Corporation)*

This truck's turrets can shoot a powerful stream of water or foam over distances of up to three hundred feet. *(George Sullivan)*

emergency exits. Once the people have been evacuated, fire fighters concentrate on extinguishing the rest of the fire.

Airport fire and rescue teams receive special training that distinguishes them from city fire fighters. They have to learn where the fuel is stored on aircraft of many different types and where aircraft emergency exits are located. "City fire fighters are trained to fight structural fires and use water. We have to know how to fight fuel fires with foam," says Captain Stephen Brown at LaGuardia.

High mobility is their greatest concern. "Once the alarm sounds, we have to be able to reach the farthest part of the runway in less than three minutes," says Captain Brown. "That's an FAA requirement.

"We conduct inspections of our vehicles and other equipment on a regular basis. Every shift begins with a readiness drill.

"And the men and women in our command are constantly taking refresher courses at 'burn sites,' actually fighting simulated aircraft fires. Our training never stops."

THE BIRDMAN OF JFK

M. O. Chevalier, a Supervisor of Bird Control at John F. Kennedy International Airport in New York, is nicknamed Sammy. "But," he says, "everyone calls me the Birdman."

Like the seven other employees that make up JFK's Bird Control Unit, Sammy spends most of each of his eight-hour shifts behind the wheel of a yellow-and-white pickup truck, patrolling the airport's runways and taxiways for seagulls and other aquatic birds that nest only a few hundred feet away in the marshes that border the airport.

Anytime he spots roosting birds, Sammy sounds the horn repeatedly. If blowing the horn doesn't chase the birds away, he'll stop the truck, take the shotgun from its dashboard rack, get out, and fire the gun in the birds' direction.

The gun fires shellcrackers. Like Fourth of July fireworks, shellcrackers are explosive devices that produce a loud noise and a bright, sudden display of light. One firing usually sends the birds on their way.

Sammy's pickup truck is also equipped with a cassette player that broadcasts bird distress calls through a loudspeaker. "When a flock hears it," says Sammy, "they sense that one of their group is in trouble, and away they go. It's a quick way to get them off a runway."

Birds represent a serious and constant threat to planes at airports all over the world. A bird sucked into the jet engine of an aircraft taking off can cause a dangerous stall. A bird that smashes into a plane's windshield can injure or even kill the pilot or copilot. Airport managers have to be constantly on the alert for bird problems and be ready to take steps to solve them.

In the early days of commercial aviation, birds were seldom a hazard because they were able to get out of the way of the relatively slow-moving planes. Not anymore. The tremendous speed of today's jets, combined with their enormous size, makes collisions between birds and planes unavoidable.

According to the Fish and Wildlife Service, an agency of the U.S. Department of the Interior, pilots annually report more than fourteen hundred bird "strikes," the term used to describe a collision between a bird and any part of an aircraft. While most are not serious, bird strikes cause millions of dollars in damage to planes each year.

For decades, airport managers and airline officials didn't take bird strikes very seriously. Then on November 12, 1975, at JFK Airport, an Overseas National Airlines DC-10 bound for London raced down a runway and struck a big flock of seagulls. Several were drawn into the engine on the right wing. Vibrating crazily, the engine fell from the plane. Flames exploded from the leaking fuel.

The pilot managed to bring the huge plane to a halt at the end of the runway. Fortunately, the 139 passengers were airline employees. They had been given training in how to escape down the plane's emergency chutes, which they managed to do before the aircraft became almost completely engulfed in flames. Since that incident, birds and the hazards they present have been taken very seriously.

Gulls are involved in as many as 80 to 90 percent of all strikes. To Sammy, an enthusiastic birder—one who enjoys observing and identifying birds—they're not merely gulls. They're herring gulls, black-back gulls, ring-bill gulls, or any one of a number of other gull species.

The worst are the laughing gulls, Sammy says. A huge colony nests in Joco Marsh, just a quarter of a mile beyond JFK's Bay Runway.

Dozens of strikes occur at JFK each month, and about half of them involve laughing gulls. Sammy and his colleagues come upon their carcasses on the runway shoulders and the runways themselves.

Gulls are diurnal, Sammy points out. They're active only by day; they sleep at night. So they're never much of a problem once the sun sets.

And the laughing gull, unlike most other gull species, is

At New York's Kennedy Airport, laughing gulls are a constant hazard to aircraft taking off and landing. *(Bureau of Sport Fisheries & Wildlife)*

INSET: **To scare away birds at JFK Airport, Sammy Chavalier's shotgun fires shellcrackers, which explode like Fourth of July firecrackers.** *(George Sullivan)*

migratory. It arrives at Joco Marsh, from regions to the south, in April and remains in the area until September.

While gulls are implicated in a vast majority of all bird strikes, other species of birds are also involved. In just one year at JFK, the Bird Control Unit recovered the bodies of kestrels, harriers, short-eared owls, a glossy ibis, a burrowing owl, and several species of ducks.

When birds become pests or hazards, airport managers first try to get them to go elsewhere. This usually involves attempting to eliminate their food supply or roosting areas—usually trees, ponds, or marshes.

Sometimes an airport manager will call upon a specialist in the scientific study of birds for help. Ornithologists, as they are called, can provide airport authorities with useful information about problem birds. Besides identifying the species, an ornithologist can explain the bird's diet and habitat, its migrating movements, and flight patterns.

One winter several years ago, the manager of the Newark (New Jersey) International Airport turned to an ornithologist when the airport was besieged by thousands of starlings. The ornithologist soon discovered that the starlings liked to roost in Norway pines that grew near the passenger terminal and parking lots. The trees had been planted very close together, the way roosting birds like them. When the trees were thinned out, the birds left.

If such tactics don't work, or simply don't apply to the area, the next step is to keep annoying the birds until they decide to depart, even if it's only for a short span of time. Noisemaking devices are common. The Bay Runway at JFK, more than two miles in length, is lined with a dozen Scare-away cannons that explode periodically. Fueled by propane gas and fitted with an igniter that explodes a regulated amount of the gas periodically, the cannons were originally used by farmers to chase away birds from valuable crops.

Asked about the effectiveness of such cannons, Sammy Chevalier shrugs. "After two or three explosions," he says, "the birds get used to them.

"There's no cure-all," Sammy adds. "The cannons are only effective when used along with everything else. You have to use the horn in the truck, the distress calls from the tape deck, the shotgun, and the shellcrackers—everything."

Using live ammunition is another alternative. "Even though the gulls are a protected species, we have a permit from the Fish and Wildlife Service to shoot them," Sammy points out. "It was issued in the interest of public safety, to insure the safe travel of air passengers."

Federal officials are sometimes assigned to shoot down laughing gulls. During a period between May 20 and August 8, 1991, biologists from the U.S. Agriculture Department's Animal and Plant Health Inspection Service killed

Cannons like this one, timed to explode every 10 to 20 minutes, line the Bay Runway at JFK Airport. *(George Sullivan)*

14,886 gulls at Kennedy Airport. Almost all were laughing gulls. The shooting took place during the gulls' breeding season.

Naturalists were angry over the shooting. Some questioned whether it would produce the desired results. "The bird population is so high that the shooting should not have a significant impact as a one-time action," said John T. Tanacredi, an official with the National Park Service. But Mr. Tanacredi added that the program could have an effect if it occurred each year. In 1992, the program was resumed.

To Sammy Chevalier, killing the birds is no solution. "If you killed a thousand birds today, they'd be replaced by another thousand in the next week or so."

Another tactic is to attempt to poison some of the birds, especially if there are large numbers involved. Chemicals are available that, when mixed with their food, cause birds to act erratically or cry out in distress. This behavior by a small number can cause entire flocks to abandon their feeding or roosting sites.

In recent years, the Environmental Protection Agency (EPA), out of their concern about the harmful side effects of toxic chemicals, has put strict limits on the poisoning of nuisance birds. The public's health is at stake, the EPA believes. Such chemicals can be applied only by individuals licensed by the EPA.

For any airport near water or a landfill, birds remain a deadly hazard. About the only real solution to the problem is to rely on a mobile runway patrol, staffed by dedicated individuals, men and women who are equipped with a wide variety of bird annoyance devices. "The whole combination is the only way to go," says Sammy Chevalier.

SHELTER FOR ANIMALS

New York's John F. Kennedy Airport is the sixth busiest airport in the United States and the eighth busiest in the world, handling almost 30 million passengers a year (about double the number for which it was built). But these statistics refer only to JFK's human air travelers. The airport is also a major transfer point for traveling animals. The animals are housed at JFK's Animalport, the only facility of its kind in North America.

A fireproof, soundproof two-story building, just minutes away from the airport's busy airline terminals, the Animalport has been sheltering animals entering and leaving the United States, plus those in-between domestic flights, since 1958, the year it was founded by the American Society for the Prevention of Cruelty to Animals (ASPCA). The Animalport is open 24 hours a day, 365 days a year.

Each year, the Animalport's professionally trained staff feeds, walks, exercises, and provides loving care for about fifteen thousand guests. There are tiled kennels for cats and dogs, spacious stalls for horses, cattle, sheep, and other livestock, and temperature-controlled rooms for tropical birds and other exotic animals.

Some of the Animalport's more unusual guests have included Ling-Ling, China's celebrity panda, and the polo ponies that belong to Great Britain's Prince Charles. The Animalport has also sheltered lions, polar bears, elephants, giraffes, storks, and spiders. A special kitchen makes it possible to satisfy the wide range of dietary needs such animals represent.

ABOVE LEFT: **Kathi Travers, director of JFK's Animalport, poses with Squeaky, a squirrel monkey and a frequent Animalport guest.** *(George Sullivan)*

ABOVE RIGHT: **JFK's Animalport offers tiled kennels for dogs and cats, plus stalls for horses, cattle, sheep, and other livestock.** *(George Sullivan)*

"Once, when we boarded a sea lion named Tuesday overnight, we needed herring," recalls Kathi Travers, the Animalport's director. "The only herring in my neighborhood comes with sour cream from a delicatessen. So I went to the city aquarium in Brooklyn. I said to the director, 'I've come to borrow, not a cup of sugar, but a bucket of herring.' He was happy to grant my request.

"When we had Russian circus bears here, I went shopping for them in the local supermarket. I got honey, cookies, and black pumpernickel bread."

In the case of cats, dogs, and other household pets, the Animalport staff members ask individual owners what they've been feeding their pets, and then try to duplicate the diet. "We have some owners," says Ms. Travers, "who bring us special foods for their dogs and cats."

When the Animalport is called upon to shelter an exotic animal species, Ms. Travers calls New York's Bronx Zoo for advice on housing and what to feed it. "The Bronx Zoo is great," she says. "But if I can't get an expert there, I'll call the San Diego Zoo or the Los Angeles Zoo." Veterinarians are on call at all times at the Animalport.

Ms. Travers, the Animalport's director since 1987, campaigns constantly for the humane transport of animals. The chief offenses she's on guard against are putting animals in undersized crates, underfeeding them, tranquilizing them with drugs, or subjecting them to extreme heat or cold. It also upsets her to see animals being transported in flatbed trucks or being loaded or unloaded by means of steeply inclined conveyor belts.

"When animals are traveling and they're away from their owners, they're under a lot of stress," Ms. Travers says. "We want to eliminate as much stress as possible."

When your pet travels in an airline cargo system, the ASPCA offers these suggestions:

- Purchase a well-constructed, well-ventilated shipping container. Be sure it provides sufficient room for your pet to stand, turn around, and lie down. Shipping crates are available at most pet shops and from the airlines.

- Line the container with shredded paper. Include one of the pet's favorite toys and a small article of clothing that bears your scent.
- A few days before departure, start getting the pet accustomed to the container. Feed the pet in the container or allow the pet to use it as a bed.
- Feed the pet a light meal at least six hours before departure. Water for the pet can spill during loading. Freeze water in a plastic cup, the type in which margarine or whipped butter comes packed, and attach it inside the container. The ice will have melted by the time the pet gets thirsty.
- Information as to the pet's destination—name, address, and telephone number—should be secured to the top of the crate. The pet should also be wearing an identification tag bearing your name, address, and telephone number on its collar.

Containers for shipping pets should be well-constructed and well-ventilated, with enough room for the pet to stand, turn around, and lie down. *(George Sullivan)*

5

Controlling Air Traffic

A Boeing 727-200 with 125 passengers aboard moves slowly along a taxiway onto the holding apron of Runway 13 at LaGuardia Airport in New York. At the far end of the runway, another jet is lifting into the air, its three engines screaming, each spewing a trail of dark smoke.

The 727-200 captain, who has already been thoroughly briefed on weather conditions and the best route to take, rechecks the flight plan to Chicago's O'Hare Airport. He glances through the window to the air traffic control tower about half a mile away, then nods to the copilot, who presses a microphone button and says, "LaGuardia Tower, American Airlines 321, ready for takeoff on Runway 13."

From the "cab," the circular glass-walled room atop LaGuardia's 10-story tower, an air traffic controller says, "American Airlines 321, taxi into position and hold." The three-engine jet makes a right turn onto Runway 13 and stops.

The controller checks the green-glowing radar screen and

61

ABOVE LEFT: **The air traffic control tower at New York's LaGuardia Airport** (*George Sullivan*)

ABOVE RIGHT: **From their glass-walled perch, tower controllers get a panoramic view of runways and taxiways.** (*Federal Aviation Administration*)

then looks out onto the expanse of crisscrossing runways and taxiways that make up LaGuardia Airport. Although the radar indicates all is clear, he wants to double-check that no plane is landing on the runway that intersects Runway 13, that the taxiways that cross it are not in use, and that no airport vehicles are in the area. He speaks into his microphone. "American Airlines 321, cleared for takeoff," he says.

The pilot advances the throttles. The silvery jet roars to life and then begins racing down the seven-thousand-foot runway. The pilot pulls back on the U-shaped control wheel called the yoke. The plane's elevators, control surfaces built into the tail, go up. Easing into the air, American Flight 321 quickly begins to climb over Flushing Bay and New York's borough of Queens.

"American 321, contact departure control," the tower controller says. The copilot moves a dial that changes the radio's frequency. "LaGuardia departure control," says the copilot, "American 321 is with you."

Every day of the year in some 325 operating towers, air traffic controllers handle more than two hundred thousand takeoffs and landings at airports across the nation. They are responsible for the safety of half a billion airline passengers a year.

Controllers may work in the glass-enclosed room at the top of the tower, in the darkened room below it, or in a nearby building. But they have the same goal: to provide for the safe separation and movement of landing, departing, and maneuvering aircraft.

As of 1991, there were between fourteen thousand and fifteen thousand air traffic controllers. About nine thousand worked in airport towers.

Thousands of others serve as arrival and departure controllers. Hunched over radar screens, they guide planes that are from five to thirty-five miles from the airports.

Still other controllers work at the nation's 24 en route centers, known officially as Air Route Traffic Control Centers, or ARTCCs. These controllers keep a constant check on aircraft operating on established airways, the invisible pathways that crisscross the nation's airspace.

In the New York City area, approach controllers are

Approach controllers, bent over radarscopes, work in dimly lit rooms.
(Federal Aviation Administration)

based at the Terminal Radar Approach Center (TRACON) in Garden City, New York, on Long Island, about 22 miles east of LaGuardia Airport. The New York TRACON (pronounced TRAY-con) not only controls aircraft departing from and arriving at LaGuardia; it is responsible for all aircraft within an area of twenty-one thousand square miles, covering parts of four states—New York, New Jersey, Connecticut, and Pennsylvania.

Within that area are the control towers of three major airports—LaGuardia, JFK, and Newark—and forty-seven

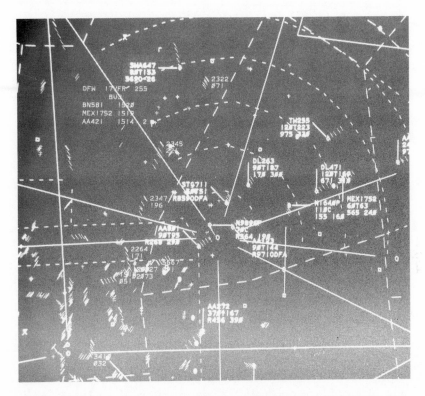

On a controller's radar screen, airplanes appear as small "blips" about the size of a grain of rice. Each blip has its own identifying "tag." *(Federal Aviation Administration; S. Michael McKean)*

smaller ones. Besides approaches and departures, the TRACON controllers are also responsible for planes over-flying the huge area.

Other TRACONS, providing radar coverage for several airports in one general area, are located in Chicago, Dallas/ Fort Worth, Oakland (California), and many other cities. But New York's TRACON is the busiest operation of its kind. In fact, about one out of every ten airplane flights in the United States arrives, departs, or overflies airspace controlled by the New York TRACON.

*   *   *

As American Airlines Flight 321 continues to gain altitude, New York TRACON hands off responsibility for the flight to an en route center in Ronkonkoma, New York, also on Long Island. Soon after, Flight 321 reaches its cruising altitude of thirty-two thousand feet.

The next handoff occurs when the controller in Ronkonkoma Center transfers responsibility to the en route Cleveland Center, located in Oberlin, Ohio. The Cleveland controller, in turn, hands off the flight to a colleague at the Chicago en route center in Aurora, Illinois.

When Flight 321 is about 30 miles from O'Hare Airport, the Chicago en route controller transfers responsibility to Chicago TRACON. A controller there lines up the plane for its final approach into O'Hare.

Responsibility for Flight 321 passes to the control tower at O'Hare when the aircraft is about six miles from the runway. An O'Hare controller then monitors the plane's landing. The last handoff is made to a ground controller, who directs the plane to its assigned gate.

LOOKING BACK

In the early days of scheduled air transportation, no one sought to control planes from the ground, to guide them as they moved through the sky, landed, or took off. Pilots were on their own.

There were so few planes flying in the 1920s that air traffic was not a problem. But even if it had been, there were no electronic control systems available with the ability to keep track of aircraft in the sky.

A pilot in those days navigated from one point to another

simply by looking down at known landmarks—roads or railroad tracks, lakes or rivers, familiar towns, or mountain peaks.

Contact flying, as it was called, was a satisfactory method of getting from one place to another, except when the weather turned bad and clouds obscured the ground. The pilot then had two choices: either fly "over the top," above the cloud cover, or below it, a strategy known as "hedgehopping." This put the pilot and the plane close to the ground and increased the risk of colliding with a church steeple or mountaintop.

Going over the top was just as hazardous. After flying over the clouds for any length of time, unable to see any visual reference points, the pilot would often lose his sense of direction. Such a flight usually ended with an emergency landing, perhaps in a farmer's field or along a strip of dirt road.

It is no wonder that during the period from 1922 to 1925, one pilot was killed for every ten thousand miles of flying. If pilot deaths occurred at the same rate today, the fatalities for a year would be in the thousands.

The sophisticated air traffic control system in use today has its roots in the 1920s when pilots began to rely on scattered radio stations and rotating floodlights—light beacons—to get from one landing field to the next. During periods of poor visibility, of course, the light beacons were of little or no value.

Air navigation took a giant step forward during the early 1930s with the introduction of the radio beam. From an airport, a focused beam of radio signals was sent out to guide the plane. Received by the pilot in his earphones, the radio beam was like an invisible highway in the sky. All the pilot had to do was keep the plane on the beam, and he would eventually reach the airport from which it was being sent.

Radio beams were less than perfect, however. Tall mountains or static electricity could and did interfere with the signal, confusing the pilot. Long after radio beams were in use, many pilots, because they lacked confidence in the new method of navigation, continued to hedgehop.

Radio ranges were another step forward. These were radio stations established along airways that the pilot heard as he passed over them. He could use a radio range to determine a plane's position—get a "fix"—along the airway. In some cases, he was able to communicate with the range, reporting his position.

As the number of planes increased, pilots started to compete for airspace, especially near busy air terminals. Traffic control began to loom as a problem. Imagine a busy downtown intersection without any traffic lights.

Some authority was needed to establish rules and regulations, and to enforce them. On July 6, 1936, the Bureau of Air Commerce of the Department of Commerce took control of the nation's air traffic.

Two years later, the Civil Aeronautics Act brought the Civil Aeronautics Authority (CAA) into existence. The CAA was later divided into two agencies: the Civil Aeronautics Board, responsible for accident investigation, and the Civil Aeronautics Administration, responsible for air traffic control.

More recently, in 1958, the Federal Aviation Act created the Federal Aviation Agency (FAA), to replace the earlier agencies. The FAA was given responsibility for air navigation and traffic control. The FAA was renamed the Federal

Aviation Administration in 1967 and placed in the newly created Department of Transportation.

Meanwhile, important technical developments had been taking place. Radar, developed during World War II, transformed the science of air traffic control. With radar, controllers at towers and in en route centers could determine the precise location of aircraft in the air and track them as they moved.

The radar used by tower controllers is called Airport Surveillance Radar, or ASR. It tells each controller the actual position of all aircraft within 50 miles of the tower.

Each airplane appears as a "blip" about the size of a grain of rice on the radar screen. Beneath the blip, there is an identity tag for each aircraft, two lines of coded information that report the name of the airline, the flight number, and the aircraft's speed and altitude. This information is generated by electronic equipment aboard the plane, received at the control center, and there digitized by computers.

Of course, no controller can do his or her job without radio communications. Radio is what links controllers with pilots.

ILS

To help bring planes down safely, the control tower relies on an electronic aid known as the Instrument Landing System (ILS). It has been in service at American airports for more than half a century and is widely used throughout the world.

The ILS localizer beacon sends out an electronic beam that activates a needle on the aircraft's instrument panel and guides the pilot toward the runway centerline. The signal is actually an electronic extension of the centerline.

The ILS also sends out a second electronic signal to guide the plane on its sloping descent to the runway. Called a glidescope transmitter, and set to one side of the runway, it activates a second needle on the airplane's instrument panel. This signal guides the aircraft down at an even rate as it approaches the runway.

As the plane is descending, the two needles serve to indicate to the pilot whether he or she is to the right or left, or above or below—or directly on—the correct approach path to the airport. If his or her path isn't quite right, the pilot makes the necessary adjustment.

The ILS does even more. As the aircraft is descending on the glidescope, it passes through two electronic "markers." These take the form of vertical beams that penetrate the localizer, form glidescope beams, and report to the pilot the plane's precise geographical position.

The first of these, known as the outer marker, is located from five to seven miles from the end of the runway. Its beam activates a flashing blue light on the instrument panel. That tells the pilot that the plane is about twelve hundred feet above the ground, a fact the pilot can then check with the altimeter, an instrument that reports how high the plane is flying. The outer marker also sends an audio signal—two low beeps per second—that alerts the pilot as to the plane's position on the glidescope.

The aircraft continues its descent. At a distance of about thirty-five hundred feet from the end of the runway, almost three quarters of a mile, the plane passes through the middle marker. An amber light flashes on the instrument panel,

A glideslope antenna for an ILS—instrument landing system *(Federal Aviation Administration)*

and the pilot hears a series of long and short high-pitched beeps. These indicate to the pilot that the plane should be approximately seven hundred feet above the ground.

Seconds later, the pilot sees the runway approach lights. It's a critical moment. The plane is at what's called "decision height." It's at this instant that the pilot must decide whether it's safe to land or whether he or she should pull up, abort the landing, and go around to try again.

During daylight hours when skies are clear, there's no

need to use instruments to bring planes down. Pilots prefer to make visual approaches and landings. But should the weather begin to deteriorate, a tower controller switches on the ILS system. Controllers also monitor the system to see that it is operating properly.

In the years ahead, ILS is to be replaced by a Microwave Landing System (MLS). This will be able to locate the aircraft several miles from the airport and actually fly it to a safe landing by operating the plane's automatic pilot system.

IN THE TOWER

At major airports, several controllers, each with a different set of responsibilities, are on duty at one time in the control

A lighted pathway helps guide pilots on visual approaches. *(Federal Aviation Administration)*

tower. Some monitor radarscopes; others scan runways and taxiways, issuing orders to pilots.

It is a calm and businesslike atmosphere, like being in a small and efficient office. While each controller has his or her own set of responsibilities, they all must work together as a team. They are careful and methodical.

No two tower operations are exactly alike. At a small airport, controllers may handle only a few flights an hour. At a major airport, it's much different. At O'Hare in Chicago or at Dallas/Fort Worth, as many as two hundred flights can land and take off within an hour.

Rush hours in the sky can cause a great deal of stress. Rain and fog, which cut visibility, also increase the tension. "It can get exciting," says one controller, "better than any video game."

The person known as the local controller is responsible for departures and arrivals. He or she gives pilots instructions for landings and takeoffs and also provides weather information. "Delta four thirty-three, reduce speed to one seven zero," the controller says firmly. Delta 433 acknowledges the order. "United eight forty, turn right, one two zero," the controller says.

Controllers do not stay in front of their radarscopes for more than two hours at a time. There are frequent breaks.

Another controller is responsible for the terminal control area. Hunched over a radar screen and watching dozens of blips, his or her job is to keep track of small planes and helicopters in the area, making sure none presents a hazard to the commercial aircraft.

A third controller transfers aircraft to an en route controller when the aircraft leave the tower's airspace. That controller also receives control of flights coming into the tower's airspace.

The ground controller, also stationed in the tower, directs not only aircraft on runways and taxiways, but also any vehicles that enter the runway area. He or she may rely upon Airport Surface Detection Equipment (ASDE), a type of radar.

"Sometimes a pilot will ask us to check whether his plane's landing gear is down or whether a hatch is securely closed," says Fred Maass, **an air traffic controller at New York's LaGuardia Airport. "That's when we use binoculars."** *(George Sullivan)*

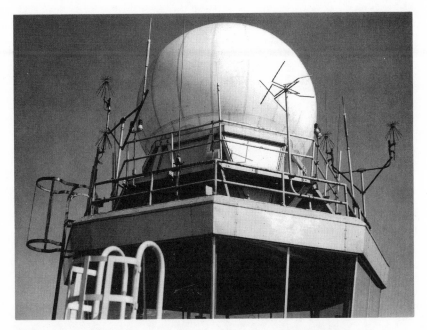

This bulbous structure atop the control tower houses ASDE—Airport Surface Detection Equipment. *(Federal Aviation Administration)*

The year 1990 was not a good one for tower controllers. There were runway crashes in Atlanta and Detroit. Nineteen ninety-one was even worse. Early that year, a runway collision in Los Angeles between a USAir jetliner and a smaller commuter plane killed 34 people.

In the months that followed the crash, the Federal Aviation Administration announced important changes in equipment and procedures, in an effort to reduce the risk of ground collisions. Runway and taxiway signs and their markings were to be standardized as to their color, size, size of letters and numerals, and lighting. The FAA also began testing an improved ground radar system that helps controllers keep track of taxiing aircraft and sounds a warning if a collision might occur.

GETTING TRAINED

Although no college education is required to become an air traffic controller, the job does require a certain type of skill. You have to be good at "getting the picture." From the blips presented on the radarscope, you have to be able to visualize the relationships these blips have to one another in three dimensions.

Persons who are skilled in chess or bridge, a card game, make good controllers, it's said. In both chess and bridge, the ability to plan moves in advance is critical to winning.

"You have to be able to work with other people," says Robert Rosscoe, Air Traffic Manager at LaGuardia Airport

About four percent of air traffic controllers are women. *(Federal Aviation Administration; S. Michael McKean)*

in New York. "You also have to be confident in your ability and be able to project your confidence through the radio. This means being fairly aggressive with pilots and taking command of the situation."

Candidates for jobs as air traffic controllers are given a written test at one of the regional offices of the FAA. Those who pass the test are interviewed and given medical and psychological examinations.

Successful candidates go on to several months of training at the FAA Academy in Oklahoma City, Oklahoma. Those who complete the training program are assigned to an air traffic control facility to begin on-the-job training. At first, trainees assist controllers. Later, under supervision, they direct aircraft.

At the beginning of the 1990s, most air traffic controllers were men in their thirties. At the time, women made up about 4 percent of the workforce.

Beginners in the field earn around thirty thousand dollars a year. A veteran controller can earn as much as ninety thousand dollars a year with overtime.

It takes one to three years for a controller candidate to become what is called a Full Performance Level Controller. But fewer than half of all trainees ever achieve that status. About 40 percent fail to get passing grades at the Oklahoma City training center. Another 16 percent flunk out during their period of on-the-job training.

If the training seems tough, says the FAA, it's because it *is* tough. After all, an airplane's safe flight depends on the ability of traffic controllers to make the right decisions. These are decisions that affect the lives of nearly 2 million air travelers every day.

— 6 —

Watching the Weather

As Delta Airlines Flight 191, a wide-bodied Lockheed L1011, approached runway 17 at Dallas/Fort Worth International Airport on a Friday afternoon early in August 1985, the sky became so dark passengers couldn't see out the windows. Heavy rain pelted the plane, and lightning zigzagged in the sky.

Suddenly, the big jet, carrying 160 passengers and crew members, nosedived, bounced along the ground several times, hit cars, and exploded. Somehow 31 people, including three flight attendants, managed to survive the crash.

Flight 191 was the first major crash at the Dallas/Fort Worth Airport and the worst in Texas history. A team of investigators from the National Transportation Safety Board rushed to the scene. From the beginning, it seemed obvious that the weather had played a major role in the disaster.

Some witnesses reported seeing Flight 191 struck by lightning. But a spokesperson for the National Transportation Safety Board doubted that lightning caused the crash.

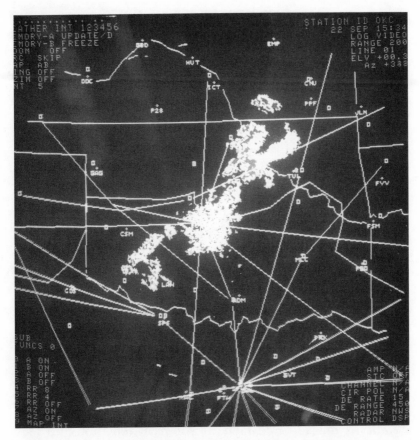

A radar screen at Fort Worth (Texas) Air Route Traffic Control Center shows a line of weather moving through Oklahoma City. *(Federal Aviation Administration)*

"Lightning doesn't normally take an airplane down," he said. "It hasn't happened in many, many years."

The more likely suspect was wind shear, an invisible, violent downdraft that often occurs during a thunderstorm. Wind shear is nearly impossible to handle during takeoff or landing. A plane that gets caught in its grip, even a jumbo jet, can be dashed to the ground in the blink of an eye.

Wind shear was a factor in at least 27 commercial aircraft accidents between 1964 and 1982, according to government studies. The most notable was the crash of a Pan American 727 after takeoff from New Orleans in 1982, an accident that left 153 dead.

President Ronald Reagan once came close to being involved in a wind shear incident. He was aboard Air Force One on August 18, 1983, when it landed at Andrews Air Force Base in Maryland. Minutes before his plane touched down, wind shear had flattened trees at the airport.

On the day of the crash of Flight 191 at Dallas/Fort Worth in 1985, the only warning might have come from numerous anemometers that were in use. These instruments, used to measure the wind's speed, could have tipped off the control tower as to the sudden changes in wind velocity.

But no warning was broadcast to Flight 191. And even if the crew had been alerted, it's not likely the pilot would have had time to react. "There's no airplane that can survive that downdraft," Captain George Berg, a veteran pilot, told *Newsweek* magazine. "Maybe if you're at ten thousand feet; but if you're at five hundred feet, there's no way."

The Federal Aviation Administration is requiring that all U.S. commercial airliners be equipped with wind-shear-detecting equipment. The equipment costs as much as fifty thousand dollars per plane. While it doesn't signal wind shear until the aircraft is already in it, even a few seconds of warning can give a skilled pilot a chance.

THE AIRPORT WEATHER STATION

Many major airports have their own weather stations, staffed by several meteorologists, men and women who

**This tower holds instruments to measure wind direction
and speed.** *(Federal Aviation Administration)*

study the atmosphere in order to be able to understand and forecast the weather. Wind shear is only one of their many concerns. Heavy fog can prevent planes from taking off or landing. Heavy snow can close down runways. A thunderstorm and its turbulence mean a rough flight. Tail winds can speed up flights; head winds slow flights down.

In bad weather, federal regulations require that planes be spaced more widely apart when taking off and landing. Long delays for passengers are the usual result.

At some airports, bad weather causes more serious problems than at others. Denver's Stapleton International Airport had a reputation as a bottleneck. During Denver's long snowy winters, delays at Stapleton sometimes caused backups from coast-to-coast. That's because Stapleton had only a limited amount of space for handling delayed aircraft. Denver relieved the problem by replacing Stapleton with the new Denver International Airport.

Most people think of meteorologists in terms of television and radio forecasts. However, the people who predict weather for the electronic media often do little more than repeat forecasts made by meteorologists who work for the National Weather Service.

Of the nation's twenty thousand or so meteorologists, about 10 percent are employed by the National Weather Service (NWS), which is part of the National Oceanic and Atmospheric Administration (NOAA) of the United States Department of Commerce. Other meteorologists work for the commercial airlines, weather consulting firms, aerospace companies, and, in some cases, television and radio stations.

At Suitland, Maryland, near Washington, D.C., the National Weather Service operates its National Meteorological

Center, its computer complex. There, the Analysis and Forecast, Computation, and Extended Forecast branches analyze climate information from the NWS's approximately three hundred weather stations and also many thousands of substations.

Satellites and weather balloons also contribute information that goes toward making weather maps. Satellites carry television cameras that take pictures showing the patterns of clouds above the earth. Picture signals are transmitted to stations on the ground, where photographs are prepared. By studying the photographs, meteorologists can get an idea where dangerous storms might be developing.

Weather balloons measure conditions in the upper atmosphere. They report temperature, air pressure, and humidity at various levels up to ninety thousand feet. They also track the direction and speed of winds aloft. With the aid of high-speed computers, meteorologists at the NWS's Suitland, Maryland, headquarters use much of the information collected to make weather maps. They prepare weather maps of the nation, the North American continent, and the world. Simplified versions of these maps are often used in TV weather forecasts and printed in newspapers.

The maps are also sent by a facsimile service to airport weather stations. "We get two hundred to three hundred maps a day from the National Center," says Gene Hathaway, official in charge of the NWS station at Newark Airport in New Jersey. "Even though we don't print them all, we'd be pretty much out of business were it not for Suitland.

"For instance, we provide packets of weather information to some of the airlines that fly internationally. These packets include maps for winds aloft, so the pilot can plan the

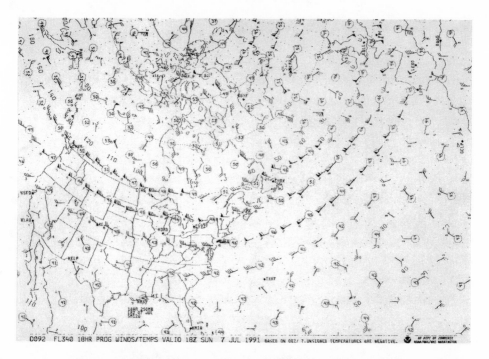

The captain of a flight from New York to Lisbon, Portugal, received this weather map, which shows the wind's speed and direction over the Atlantic Ocean. *(National Weather Service)*

speediest route and also be able to navigate around severe weather. Well, without the maps from Suitland, we'd be giving them blank sheets of paper in many cases."

While the forecasts prepared at National Meteorological Center are quite accurate in predicting general conditions in the atmosphere, they are less reliable in predicting the weather over a certain runway at a specific time. Local weather conditions change rapidly. So airport meteorologists have to keep a careful watch on local conditions, cloud cover, wind, temperature, and all the rest.

"Every day is different," says Harry Woodworth, an NWS

meteorologist at Newark Airport. "Mother Nature dictates the type of work we do."

Sometimes the work can be very stressful. "At a small weather station, during the early morning hours, or on Saturday or Sunday, you might be on duty all by yourself," says Woodworth. "Suddenly a squall line begins to develop. It can be more than a hundred miles long. It brings violent gusts of wind, and often rain, snow, or sleet.

"You get very busy. You have to keep the tower informed about the storm and its characteristics. The phones start ringing. People in nearby communities want to know how serious the storm is and when it's going to end.

"And every half hour you have to go out on the roof and measure how much precipitation you've had.

"If it's a snowstorm, the people doing runway snow removal want half-hourly reports on the amount of the snow that's fallen and how much more is expected to fall.

"In the case of heavy rain, when it reaches a certain level, it's up to you to issue flood warnings to local communities. You have a lot of responsibility."

FORECASTING EQUIPMENT

In aviation's early days, the principal weather instrument found at airports was the wind sock, also called a wind cone or wind sleeve. Used to indicate the direction of the wind and also give some idea of its intensity, the wind sock takes the form of a tapered cloth tube, open at both ends, that rotates freely atop a tall pole. In turning to catch the wind, it automatically indicates the direction in which the wind is blowing.

Wind socks, or cones, which date to aviation's earliest times, are still in use today. *(George Sullivan)*

Wind cones are still in use today. In fact, the Federal Aviation Administration says every airport must have them. They're used chiefly by helicopter pilots or by any other aircraft that fly low and slow.

Today, weather vanes indicate the direction of the wind for airport meteorologists. Several anemometers at each airport measure wind speed.

Hygrometers measure the amount of moisture in the air.

Rain gauges, accurate to one one hundredth of an inch, measure the amount of rainfall.

The ceilometer uses a laser beam in measuring the height of cloud bases, that is, their lower edges. This is very important information to a pilot landing or taking off.

Visibility is also important. Pilots want to know the greatest possible distance they can see without instruments.

Airport meteorologists use an instrument called a transmissometer to check visibility. Located near the end of the runway, the transmissometer sends a beam of light to a nearby photoelectric cell. The cell measures the amount of light it receives. If the visibility is poor because of fog, rain, or snow, the light received by the cell is much dimmer than the light transmitted.

After measuring the amount of light it has received, the photoelectric cell sends a signal to a recording instrument in the airport weather station. Called a Runway Visual Range (RVR) indicator, the instrument reports the estimated visibility in feet at the end of the runway.

Airport weather stations use radar to help predict the passage of storms. The radar system sends out radar waves, which are reflected by raindrops in the clouds. The returning waves can be detected for a distance of up to 250 miles.

The location of the rainy area appears on a screen that resembles a television screen. By using radar, meteorologists can determine not only the direction in which a storm is moving and its speed, but also its intensity.

"The most important piece of equipment to come along in recent years is the computer," says Gene Hathaway of Newark Airport. "It enables us to compile information almost instantly that otherwise would require hours.

LEFT: **A transmissometer reports on airport visibility by sending out a beam of light to a nearby photoelectric cell, which measures the light's intensity.** *(Federal Aviation Administration)*

ABOVE: **A signal from the transmissometer is received by the weather station Runway Visual Range (RVR), which reports estimated visibility in feet.** *(George Sullivan)*

"Take the business of forecasting precipitation amounts, that is, estimating rainfall for a certain area. In the past, you'd have to go through mountains of paper to do it. Now, with a computer, it takes less than a minute."

When it comes to forecasting, today's meteorologists still do what early pilots did—look up into the sky. "You can tell a lot just by looking out the window," says Newark Airport meteorologist Harry Woodworth. "How cloudy is it? What types of clouds have formed? In what direction are they heading? Maybe you can even see a thunderstorm beginning to form.

"When it comes to forecasting, sometimes the best thing is still your eyeballs."

FUTURE FORECASTING

The federal government is developing a new, nationwide weather-tracking system so powerful it can track a swarm of insects moving across a wheat field thirty miles away. Called Nexrad, for next generation radar, the system would give airport weather stations a quicker and more accurate view of atmospheric conditions.

One of Nexrad's foremost features is a sophisticated radar—Doppler radar, named after nineteenth-century Austrian physicist and mathematician Christian Doppler. Doppler radar measures the motion of air by bouncing microwaves off the tiny droplets in the center of cloud systems and picking up their echoes.

Doppler radar may be able to warn of advancing wind shear, which pilots continue to fear more than any other atmospheric disturbance. One plan calls for 155 of the nation's airports to get Doppler radar during the 1990s.

Overhauling the nation's weather stations could cost as much as two billion dollars. But supporters of the program say the money spent will be worth it if the new equipment helps to remove weather as a cause of aviation accidents.

7

Airport Security

At the Portland (Oregon) International Airport on the evening before Thanksgiving Day in 1971, an ordinary looking, middle-aged man who called himself D. B. Cooper bought a ticket on Northwest Orient Airlines Flight 305 to Seattle. He took an aisle seat near the rear of the aircraft, a Boeing 727.

Once the plane was in the air, Cooper, wearing dark glasses, handed a folded note to flight attendant Florence Schaffer. "Read that," he said.

The note, hand printed in ink, demanded four parachutes and two hundred thousand dollars in twenty-dollar bills. The parachutes and the money were to be delivered to him when the plane landed in Seattle. Otherwise, he was going to blow up the aircraft with a bomb he was carrying in his briefcase.

Schaffer gulped and took the note to Captain William Scott. At first, Scott didn't take the threat seriously. Leaving the copilot at the controls, he went back to talk to the passenger. Cooper showed the captain what was in his briefcase—two red cylinders and a tangle of wires, what looked like some kind of explosive device. Captain Scott decided it was no joke.

After the plane landed in Seattle, the money, stuffed in a laundry sack, was turned over to Cooper along with the parachutes. In return, he released the thirty-six passengers and all but three crew members.

Cooper then demanded the plane be flown to Reno, Nevada. When it landed at Reno, there was no sign of D. B. Cooper. But the aircraft's rear exit ramp, which lowered from the underside of the aircraft, was open. Apparently Cooper, dressed in a business suit and wearing street shoes, had jumped from the plane over southwest Washington.

No trace of Cooper was ever found. In time, he became a folk hero. T-shirts with the slogan D. B. COOPER— WHERE ARE YOU? became popular. Countless articles and several books were written about the case. The town of Ariel, Washington, near where Cooper is believed to have landed, held daylong celebrations on the anniversary of the crime.

There's more to the D. B. Cooper legacy than that. When Cooper boarded Flight 305, an agent glanced at his briefcase to be sure it was small enough to be taken aboard as carry-on baggage. There was no passenger screening in those days, no X-ray scanners or metal-detectors. These are standard today, of course, and D. B. Cooper is one of the reasons they are.

The Federal Aviation Administration is responsible for aviation security, for combating air piracy, which was D. B. Cooper's crime, and sabotage. In its efforts to protect airline

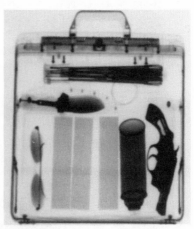

ABOVE LEFT: **Skyjacker D.B. Cooper helped trigger the use of airport X-ray scanners and metal-detectors.** *(Wide World)*

ABOVE RIGHT: **The contents of a scanned briefcase appear on a black-and-white monitor.** *(EG&G Astrophysics Research Corporation, Long Beach, California)*

passengers, the FAA oversees the security work of the airport operators and the airlines.

For decades, airports operated without electronic systems for checking passengers and their baggage. Few people saw any need for them. Then in the late 1960s, when commercial aviation was struck with a wave of hijacking, or "skyjacking," as it came to be called, attitudes toward security changed.

A skyjacker would seize control of a plane once it was airborne, then threaten to destroy it and the people aboard unless certain demands were met. Sometimes the skyjacker wanted huge sums of money. Other times, the skyjacker was seeking to flee one country for another.

Hundreds of skyjackings took place during the 1960s. Several resulted in the loss of life and destruction of the aircraft.

Many nations banded together to try to put an end to skyjacking. A treaty providing punishment for skyjacking went into effect in 1973. More than 40 nations, including the United States and Canada, agreed to support the treaty.

The same year, the federal government established certain security regulations. These required the inspection of all passengers and their baggage. These regulations, still in effect, were meant to prevent armed persons from boarding planes.

The search process begins at the counter where passengers check in for their flight. Each person's bag is placed on a conveyor belt that leads to the airline's main baggage conveyor system.

At the time it is placed on the conveyor belt, the bag is electronically weighed and X-rayed. The image produced by the X-ray appears on a TV screen, which is monitored by a specially trained operator. If a suspicious object is detected in the bag, the baggage conveyor system is immediately shut down. This suspicious object is X-rayed from several different angles and close up. If it continues to arouse suspicions, the owner of the bag is likely to be called upon to open the bag so the object can be examined.

Luggage that passengers carry aboard gets much the same kind of examination. Each bag is placed on a conveyor belt to be carried past cameras that provide an X-ray television picture of the contents. The picture is transmitted to a screen, which is monitored by security personnel.

Airline passengers are electronically searched by walking through a metal-detecting gateway. *(Federal Aviation Administration)*

Any object that appears suspicious is closely examined. In most cases, what looked like a weapon is actually something quite innocent—a camera lens, a can of aerosol spray, or an electric shaver.

Occasionally, a toy pistol or knife that has been purchased as a souvenir is discovered. In such cases, the object is taken from the owner, given to a member of the airline cabin crew for the flight, and returned to the owner when the aircraft reaches its destination.

Of course, when a real weapon is found, it's a serious matter. Police are summoned, the weapon is confiscated, and an investigation follows.

It's not merely baggage that's inspected. All passengers are electronically searched by walking through a metal-detecting gateway. These work on a simple principle. Between the gateway's metal columns, an electromagnetic field is produced. The invisible "lines" of this electromagnetic field penetrate everything within their path—paper or cloth, wood or plastic.

Metal, however, causes certain disturbances within the field. These disturbances set off a signal—a blinking light or high-pitched beep—to alert the operator of the machine.

Usually the alarm-producing objects turn out to be quite harmless. They often include costume jewelry, cigarette lighters, keys, or keyrings. In such cases, the passenger is asked to surrender the objects and pass through the gateway a second time. If no alarm sounds, his or her possessions are returned. The incident causes no concern.

Security personnel operating airport detection equipment have been trained to recognize what a typical hijacker looks like. The profile includes facial appearance, the kind of baggage the person is probably carrying, and the manner in which he or she acts during the inspection. Anyone who arouses suspicions gets a much closer examination.

Is it possible to fool a metal-detector? Possibly. A gun or a knife could be encased in a very dense material, such as lead. It would show up on the screen as a dark blob. It's then up to the security guard to order the owner to open the bag so the mysterious blob can be examined.

X-ray machines that are powerful enough to penetrate any such shielding do exist. However, they rely on a higher level of radiation than the scanners now in use. This level is so high that it fogs film and ruins magnetic tape. Security officials feel the low-power scanners are doing the job—as long as security guards keep alert and don't hesitate to inspect the contents of bags.

PREVENTING SABOTAGE

At 8:15 A.M. on June 23, 1985, Air India Flight 182, with 304 passengers and 22 crew members aboard, was nearing the end of a quiet trip across the North Atlantic from Toronto. The Boeing 747 was bound for Bombay, India.

When the plane was about 90 miles southwest of the Irish coast, the captain called air traffic control at Shannon Airport. He asked for permission to overfly Shannon on the way to a refueling stop at Heathrow Airport in London. It was a routine communication.

Air traffic controllers at Shannon tracked the plane as it headed for its approach into Heathrow. Then suddenly, without the slightest warning, Flight 182 vanished from the radar screen. "One minute it was there, and the next minute it was gone," said a bewildered air traffic controller.

Wreckage and bodies were found almost directly beneath the spot where controllers had lost the radar blip. No one survived the disaster.

All evidence pointed to an explosive decompression of the cockpit. A bomb, which Sikh terrorists claimed to have planted, is believed to have caused the disaster.

On the afternoon of the very same day, Canadian Pacific Flight 003 from Vancouver, British Columbia, Canada, arrived at Narita International Airport in Japan. The passengers and crew got off. Baggage handlers were still unloading the plane's cargo spaces when there was a blinding flash and an explosion. "Everybody heard it," said an airline employee. "It sounded like two cars colliding." Two people were killed.

As these tragedies suggest, detecting a concealed bomb is no easy matter. "A gun looks like a gun," says Robert

Beasley of the U. S. Department of Transportation. "But a bomb can come in any shape or size."

Concealed bombs are also difficult to detect because they don't have to be very big. The amount of plastic explosive material required to fatally damage an aircraft can be molded into a ball about the size of a baseball. It also can be shaped into a thin sheet and hidden within the cover of a book or the lining of a suitcase.

When it comes to detecting bombs, the nose is a better instrument than an X-ray scanner. That's because explosives give off a very distinct, although delicate, odor.

For years, dogs, who have a super sense of smell, have been used to sniff out bombs. Turn a trained dog loose in a

Dogs are often used to sniff out bombs, but sometimes they aren't reliable. *(Federal Aviation Administration)*

room in which a bomb has been planted, and he'll go right to it.

But dogs aren't perfect. They can get confused. Stand a dog by a conveyor and run suitcases past him or let him prowl through the baggage compartment of a 747, and he's likely to mix up the smell of things like shoe polish or perfume with that of explosives.

Scientists are seeking to develop devices that are as sensitive as a dog's nose in picking up smells, but with a greater degree of reliability.

There's the gas chromatograph, for example, which can identify the vapors given off by dynamite or TNT. When a sample of air is fed into the chromatograph, it is able to single out any gas particles because it takes them several seconds longer than air particles to travel a measured distance within the detector.

The instrument can identify a single particle of a bomb's explosive gas in a trillion particles of air. Unfortunately, in windblown open cargo areas, the chromatograph is unreliable, and fails to work as well as a dog's nose. Most "sniffing" detectors, such as the chromatograph, are still in the development stage.

X-ray scanners are the tried and proven method of seeking to locate concealed explosives. Scanners now in use provide a two-dimensional view of a suitcase and its contents. Advanced scanners, however, provide a three-dimensional view. These are of greater value in attempting to detect modern explosives, which are fairly dense. But three-dimensional scanners are more complex and more costly.

Neutron scanners have also been tried. They get high marks when it comes to detecting bombs in suitcases, but they can't be used for passenger screening because of the harmful effects of neutron radiation.

Late in 1988, the failings of airport scanning devices was again made tragically obvious. Terrorists blew up Pan Am Flight 103 over Scotland, bringing death to 270 people, including 11 people on the ground. The bomb that exploded inside the aircraft, believed to have been concealed inside a radio-cassette player, was made from a soft, puttylike material. It passed through an X-ray scanner without being detected.

The federal government reacted by passing legislation requiring major U.S. airports to install new bomb detection devices by 1993. These include X-ray systems with the ability to peek inside metal containers and zero in on plastic explosives. There are also light, portable devices, resembling vacuum cleaners, that can sniff traces of explosives on suitcases, clothing, and people. During the early 1990s, the Federal Aviation Administration began testing these and other security systems.

OTHER SECURITY MEASURES

While most airline passengers think of airport security only in terms of what happens when their baggage is screened, it is far more extensive than that. Security starts at the airport's perimeter, at the tall chain-link fence that keeps people out of what the FAA calls the "air operations area." That's where planes land, take off, and maneuver on the ground.

Security personnel on duty within these areas are instructed to follow these guidelines: If you find a door open,

ABOVE LEFT: **Police officer Adrea Dies works at the communication center at Washington's National Airport.** *(Federal Aviation Administration); Lance Strozier*

ABOVE RIGHT: **Airport perimeter security includes a chain-link fence and warning signs.** *(George Sullivan)*

lock it; an unprotected area, fence it; an area in darkness, light it; or someone you don't know, find out who it is. Such regulations are meant to keep honest people out of restricted areas. They also make it easier to spot people with harmful intentions.

Security in areas where cargo is handled has been tightened in recent years. Armed security guards are seen frequently. Remote areas and cargo storage facilities are monitored with closed-circuit TV. High value articles go into twin-lock "cages." One key is held by a security officer, the other by an airline representative. Both keys are needed to unlock the cage.

During the Persian Gulf war in 1991, the federal government, fearful of war-related terrorism, put tougher security measures into effect at airports throughout the United States. These included the towing of unoccupied cars outside terminals and the seizing of any luggage left unattended. (Terrorists are known to plant bombs in automobiles and passengers' bags.) In addition, people without tickets were no longer allowed to go beyond security checkpoints to meet passengers or see them off. There were no terrorist incidents at American airports during the war.

When the Persian Gulf war ended, the tougher security measures remained in effect. Tighter security measures mean higher costs in hiring guards and other personnel, and for screening equipment. It is the airline passengers who have to pay these costs with higher airfares.

Another part of the challenge in seeking to keep guns and bombs off planes is to do so without turning airports upside down. "There has to be a balance between perfect security and freedom of travel," says one expert in the field. "If we turn airports into armed camps, the terrorists have won."

8

"Your Flight Will Be Delayed"

To the traveler of the 1990s, most major airports are crowded and even frantic places. There are long, winding lines at ticket counters. There are lines at X-ray scanners and check-in gates, and FULL signs in airport parking lots.

Planes arrive and depart late. Sometimes flights are cancelled. Passengers spend more time fidgeting and fuming in terminals than flying.

Experts say it's likely to get worse. The rate of air travel has been growing steadily, with no end in sight.

The reason for the delays is usually congestion—too many people, too many planes. William F. Bolger, former president of the Air Transport Association, said that five out of every six delays result from millions of new passengers and the fact that there simply aren't enough airports or room at existing airports to handle them.

Scheduled airlines in the United States carry around 450 million passengers a year. That's more than twice the amount they carried during the 1970s. By the year 2000, the

Air travel today often means long lines at ticket counters and FULL signs at parking lots. *(Boston Logan International Airport)*

number is expected to be approaching 800 million, nearly double the number carried in the early 1990s.

DEREGULATION

The chief reason for the booming increase in air travel is the deregulation of the airlines. During the late 1970s, the Civil Aeronautics Board, the government agency that had regulated airline fares, routes, and schedules since 1938, began to exert less control over the industry. The idea was to encourage better service and increase competition.

Taxiway traffic jams occur frequently at most major airports. *(Federal Aviation Administration)*

Then in 1978, Congress passed the Airline Deregulation Act. The law ended the CAB's control of airline routes in 1982, and its control of fares in 1983. The CAB itself was closed down on December 31, 1984.

As a result of deregulation, many new, smaller airlines came into existence. These airlines often boasted they were "no frills" operations, lacking some of the services of the bigger, long-established airlines. They also offered fares that were considerably lower. Passenger traffic soared.

As a result of the competition, established airlines lost customers by the millions and suffered huge financial losses. But they fought back. They began offering discount fares on some routes. The great hope of airline deregulation—cheap travel—was being realized.

HUBS AND SPOKES

Another idea the major airlines adopted to boost profits was the hub-and-spokes system of routing flights. It is now a dominant feature of air travel in the United States.

A hub is the central portion of a wheel from which many spokes radiate. A hub airport is similar; it is a central point from which connecting flights to many cities radiate.

The system works like this: If you're flying south on Delta Airlines (and not going to a major city), you're almost certain to have to change planes in Atlanta, a hub airport. In fact, two-thirds of the passengers who fly into Hartsfield Atlanta Airport never visit the city of Atlanta. They're just there to change planes.

Fly to the Midwest on United Airlines, and you're likely to have to change planes in Chicago. Besides Atlanta and Chicago, major hubs are New York, Dallas/Fort Worth, Los Angeles, Minneapolis/St. Paul, and Denver.

The hub-and-spokes system may provide benefits for the airlines, but for passengers, it is often a horror show, adding extra miles and hours to the trip. Passengers used to be flown directly from one point to another, from A to B. They now fly from A to C, where they change planes for B. A trip from Cheyenne, Wyoming, to Casper, Wyoming, requires a change of planes in Denver. That more than doubles the air mileage from point to point.

To go from New York to Portland, Oregon, you have to pass through hub airports in either St. Louis or Dallas/Fort Worth, depending on which airline you choose. Either way, it adds extra miles and a great deal of time to the trip.

Experienced air travelers count on spending at least one

hour between arrival and departure in order to make their connection at the hub airport. But if the arriving plane is late, as sometimes happens, an hour is not likely to be enough time, and passengers miss their connecting flights. Some get booked on a later flight. The less fortunate don't get a flight until the next morning, meaning they must spend the night in an airport hotel.

As this suggests, the hub-and-spokes system increased the number of takeoffs and landings at hub airports. This helped to clog airways and make terminals and other passenger facilities more crowded.

The hub-and-spokes system contributes to delays, too. Bad weather is the chief cause of delays. But with hub airports, a local rainstorm can cause problems in several different cities. Suppose a passenger is sitting at O'Hare in Chicago, waiting for a flight to Boston. The passenger is told the aircraft he is supposed to take hasn't yet reached Dallas. The reason: It's still on the ground in Phoenix, because it's raining there.

By the early 1990s, 29 hub airports were in operation across the nation. While they may be bad news for passengers, they have made for shorter, better filled flights, which means greater profits for most airlines.

For the major airlines, they've produced another benefit. The smaller, upstart airlines of the 1980s, unable to afford expensive hub operations, were forced out of business.

By 1992, five airlines—American, United, Delta, Northwest, and USAir—dominated air travel in the United States. Those five handled 71 percent of all traffic. They also controlled 21 of the nation's 29 hub airports.

With less competition, the major airlines were able to control prices. The days of wild fare-cutting ended. When the big airlines did announce discounts, they usually offered them for only a small number of seats on each plane.

While the hub-and-spokes system has caused problems, very few people are calling for a return to government control of the airlines. But other solutions have been proposed. For example, a bill before Congress in 1992 would give smaller airplanes landing slots at airport gates now tightly controlled by their bigger competitors.

BIGGER AIRPLANES

Another reason airports have gotten busier is because airplanes themselves keep getting larger. In 1989, Boeing introduced the world's biggest commercial airliner, the Boeing 747-400. It offered a 16-foot longer wing than the 747-100, the first model of the plane, and 6-foot-high "winglets," angled upward and slightly outward from the wingtips.

The Boeing 747-400, introduced in 1989 and hailed as the world's biggest commercial jet, can carry as many as 566 passengers. *(Boeing)*

The new plane carries as many as 566 passengers, compared to a maximum of 385 passengers for the 747-100. By 1991, airlines of the world had ordered 412 of the Boeing 747-400. Future models of the Boeing 747 may be able to carry as many as 800 passengers.

Airbus Industrie, a European partnership that manufactures commercial aircraft, is developing new, long-range aircraft that will be capable of carrying 650 passengers.

Bigger planes are likely to mean more air travelers. For airports, they create the need for wider taxiways and for more space at gates and between gates.

During the period of enormous growth in air travel, the number of major airports in the United States stayed the same. Denver International Airport is the only major airport to be built in the United States since 1974, the year Dallas/Fort Worth International opened.

Most of today's major airports are unable to cope with the booming increase in passenger traffic. Such airports as New York's LaGuardia and Boston's Logan International were built during an era when air travel was still uncommon. Planes of that time carried many fewer passengers and used far shorter runways than today's jets. Because these airports are now hemmed in by homes and businesses, they're unable to expand.

Take O'Hare Airport in Chicago as an example. Because of its central location, O'Hare is the nation's busiest airport—and one of the most congested. It handles almost 60 million passengers and about eight hundred thousand flights a year. At peak periods, air traffic controllers at O'Hare direct up to 210 takeoffs and landings an hour.

About thirty-five thousand people work at O'Hare. The

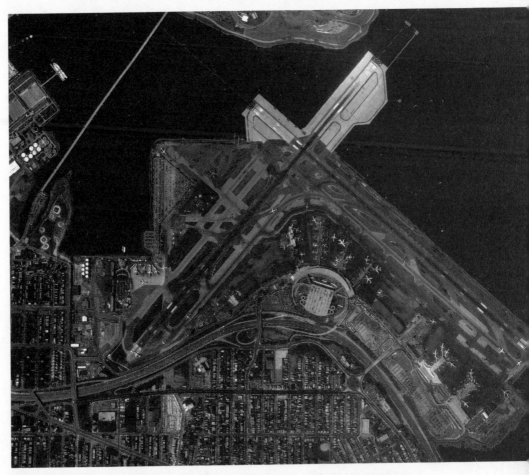

Hemmed in by homes and water, New York's LaGuardia Airport, its runways only seven thousand feet in length, has no room for expansion.
(Port Authortiy of New York and New Jersey)

seven-thousand-acre layout has three fire stations, its own police force, a post office, dozens of shops and restaurants, and a heating-and-cooling plant big enough to provide warmth and air-conditioning for a city of fifty thousand.

About all O'Hare doesn't have is room to grow. Suburbs completely surround it.

At least six other big cities—Detroit, Los Angeles, New York, Phoenix, St. Louis, and San Francisco—are also in desperate need of new airport capacity.

More than 25 airports in the United States are already overloaded, according to industry and government experts. By the year 2000, the number could be approaching 65.

SOLVING THE PROBLEM

Several remedies have been suggested. For example, the Federal Aviation Administration is looking into the possibility of opening some military airfields to commercial aircraft. El Toro Marine Corps Air Station, near Los Angeles, is one of the bases that has been suggested. Or military airfields that have been closed might be reopened and converted to use as commercial airports.

One other solution might be to build "wayports." They're also called "superhubs." These are huge airports that would be built in rural areas to be used much the way hub airports are used today, as passenger transfer points.

Air travel today often means a change of planes at a hub airport (as explained earlier in this chapter). A passenger flying west on United Airlines must often change planes in Chicago (if not heading for a major city). Going south on Delta Airlines means changing planes in Atlanta.

Wayports would be alternatives to Chicago, Atlanta, and other congested hub airports. For passengers heading from east to west, the wayport might be located in southern Illinois. For passengers going south, the wayport might be in southern Georgia.

Because the wayport uses cheaper land and does not require parking garages or an elaborate highway system (everyone arrives by air), the wayport could be built at a fraction of the cost of a regular airport.

TRAINS AS AN ALTERNATIVE

Trains have also been suggested as a way of relieving airport crowding. The idea is based on the fact that airport congestion is sometimes the result of traffic between big cities that are within a few hundred miles of one another. Travelers between these cities, it's said, could be served just as efficiently by superfast trains.

For example, business travelers between New York and Washington, or Dallas and Houston, prefer air transportation. This is also true of travelers between New York and Boston, Los Angeles and Las Vegas, and Miami, Orlando, and Tampa.

Those who propose rail transportation as a substitute for air travel between these cities point out that the French have relieved crowded airways between Paris and Lyons with what's called the T.G.V.—*train à grand vitesse,* or high-speed train. Known popularly as a bullet train, it makes the 285-mile trip in two hours. Bullet trains to link many other European cities are being planned.

In Japan, bullet trains carry about half a million passengers a day. According to Japanese Railways, some 90 percent of Japanese prefer bullet trains to other forms of transportation when making trips of three hours or less.

Those who wish to use bullet trains to link such cities as New York and Washington, or Los Angeles and Las Vegas, point to the traffic between New York and Philadelphia. Only a relatively few people fly. That's because it's so convenient and quick to travel by train between Pennsylvania Station in New York City and Philadelphia's 30th Street Station.

BUILDING NEW AIRPORTS

Perhaps the only real solution is new airports, several of them. "At least ten new airports need to be constructed over the next decade," said J. Donald Reilly, formerly executive director of the Airport Operators Council International, in 1988.

Donald R. Engan, former head of the FAA, agreed. "We know what the traffic will be," he said. "We need airports."

New airports cost about two billion dollars apiece. Where is the money to come from?

Since 1970, the federal government has been collecting a special 8 percent tax on airline tickets. This money, along with other fees, accumulates in what is called the Airport and Airways Trust Fund at the rate of about four billion dollars a year, until it is spent by Congress. Some money from the fund could go toward the construction of new airports.

Local governments could issue revenue bonds to help underwrite construction costs. For example, Denver sold about one billion dollars in bonds to help finance Denver International Airport.

The smooth operation of airports is not just a matter of passenger comfort and convenience. Better than half of air travel in the United States is for business reasons. Making airports more efficient makes good economic sense.

But the spiraling growth in air travel has overloaded our major airports, causing delays and frustration. An airport building program is what's needed, say many industry experts. The longer it's delayed, the more serious the problems are likely to become.

Glossary

air carrier airport An airport that chiefly serves the airplanes of the scheduled airlines, and also business aircraft and private planes

Air Route Traffic Control Center (ARTCC) One of the 24 centers that controls air traffic operating on established airways

Airport Surface Detection Equipment (ASDE) The radar used by controllers in directing traffic on airport runways and taxiways

Airport Surveillance Radar (ASR) A type of radar used by air traffic controllers. ASR reports the position of all aircraft within a 50-mile radius of the control tower

airway An air route for the passage of aircraft

anemometer An instrument used to measure the speed of the wind

cab The glass-walled room at the top of the air traffic control center tower that is occupied by controllers, their radar, and other equipment

ceilometer An instrument used in measuring the height of cloud bases

Civil Aeronautics Administration (CAA) A government agency that was responsible for air traffic control from 1948 until 1984

Civil Aeronautics Board (CAB) A government agency that operated from 1938 to 1984, regulating airline fares, routes, and schedules

clear zone The open area at the end of each runway used to provide aircraft with space to rise or descend

113

contact flying Navigating an airplane by visual reference to known landmarks—roads, railroad tracks, rivers, etc.

dual lane runway An airport with two pairs of parallel runways

exit taxiway See turnoff

Federal Aviation Administration (FAA) An agency of the federal government that controls air traffic; certifies aircraft, airports, pilots, and other personnel; and operates navigation aids. The FAA is part of the U.S. Department of Transportation.

fix The position of an aircraft along an airway

general aviation airport An airport that serves business aircraft and private planes. It is not available to planes of the scheduled airlines.

glidescope transmitter Part of the Instrument Landing System, an electronic signal sent to a pilot that helps to guide a landing plane on its sloping path of descent to the runway

holding area The area near the end of a runway where the plane stays as the crew makes final checks and waits for clearance from the tower to take off

holding bay A parking area near runways where planes await gate assignments or takeoff instructions

hub A centrally located airport from which connecting flights to many other airports radiate

hygrometer An instrument used to measure the amount of moisture in the air

International Air Transport Association (IATA) An organization with the goal of promoting safe, regular, and economical air transport throughout the world

Instrument Landing System (ILS) The electronic guidance system that planes use for approach and landing

jetway The telescoping walkway that joins an aircraft to the terminal

lineperson An airport worker who, using hand signals or flashlights, helps to direct an aircraft into its position at the gate

loading apron The area at a terminal gate used to park aircraft

loadsheet A statement as to an airplane's weight and balance

meteorologist A scientist who studies the atmosphere to understand and predict the weather

microwave landing system (MSL) An electronic guidance system used in automatically flying an airplane through its approach and landing

National Oceanic and Atmospheric Administration (NOAA) An agency of the Department of Commerce that gathers data, conducts research, and makes predictions concerning various aspects of the nation's environment

National Weather Service (NWS) A branch of the National Oceanic and Atmospheric Administration that provides weather forecasts and storm warnings

Nexrad An acronym for next generation radar, a new nationwide weather-watching system

radarscope The viewing screen of a radar receiver

radio range A radio station from which signals are sent to assist a pilot in keeping on course

ramp The area at a terminal gate where a plane is parked and loaded; also, the moveable staircase used for entering or leaving the cabin door of an aircraft

rapid intervention vehicle (RIV) A vehicle designed to quickly respond to airport emergencies, particularly fire and rescue operations

runway The long strip, usually paved, on which planes land and take off

runway visual range (RVR) indicator A weather station instrument that records estimated visibility at the end of a runway

scheduled airline A company that operates airplanes over fixed routes according to a timetable

taxiway A lane between a terminal gate and a runway, used by an aircraft after landing or before taking off

terminal The main airport building where passengers begin and end their flights

terminal radar approach control center (TRACON) A regional air traffic control center that handles aircraft approaches for a number of airports

transmissometer An instrument for measuring the amount of light transmitted through the atmosphere, used by meteorologists in determining visibility

turnoff A short strip of concrete or asphalt that links a taxiway and a runway; also called an exit taxiway

wayport A hub airport situated in an out-of-the-way location

wind sock A tapered cloth tube, open at both ends, that rotates at the top of a tall pole to indicate wind direction. Also called a wind cone.

Index

Page numbers in *italics* refer to photographs.

117

INDEX

Index

INDEX

Index

INDEX